CONTENT WARNINGS

This dark fantasy horroromance novella contains mature content, some of which may be troubling for readers, including: death, violence, blood, implication of homicide, and dubious consent. Please read with care—your mental health matters.

CONSUMED

MARY DUBLIN
ANNE KENDSLEY

A QUICK IRISH HISTORY LESSON

Folklore has a massive importance in Irish tradition, woven into the very legacy of the country. The fae folk are not simply whimsical fairy tales, but powerful ancient beings that are both revered and deeply feared. We want to express our gratitude to the Irish literary community for embracing new voices who want to honor and explore Irish history and mythos in fiction.

Something to note—ancient Irish culture also carried ceremonial traditions such as **handfasting**, often performed at the time of engagement as a public promise between partners. Spiritual life even pre-Christianity was deeply interwoven with society, usually led by the **druids**, who were more than priests — they were scholars, judges, poets, and keepers of sacred knowledge. Historically, texts suggest that a druid would be addressed with reverence indicating his title, i.e. "Druid (Name)."

For one of our co-authors, whose family roots run deep in Ireland, it is a place of profound personal meaning — and we take the opportunity to pen a story in this setting with great heart. We hope you enjoy!

PRONUNCIATION GUIDE

Róisín [ROH-sheen] - "LITTLE ROSE"

Niamh [NEEV] - "NYMPH" WITH LINK TO OTHERWORLDLY LANDS

Eoin [OH-in] - "BIRD," REPRESENTING FREEDOM AND THE SKIES

PLAYLIST

Bean Pháidín - CELTIC WOMAN

YOU BELONG TO ME - CAT PIERCE

BEL AIR - LANA DEL REY

ISLAND OF DOOM - AGNES OBEL

GARDEN OF MAGIC - KRISTEN LAWRENCE

THE DEATH WALTZ - TOBIAS LILJA

IDEA 22 SLOWED & REVERBED - GIBRAN ALCOCER

MAKE YOU MINE - MADISON BEER

THE FOXHUNTER - CELTIC WOMAN

LOVERS FROM THE PAST - MAREUX

SEVEN DEVILS - FLORENCE + THE MACHINE

**SCAN TO LISTEN
ON SPOTIFY**

PRAISE FOR
 CONSUMED

"A BEAUTIFUL HORROROMANCE WITH AN UNREPENTANT, MONSTROUS FMC, A VENGEFUL SENTIENT FOREST, AND AN ENDING THAT WILL LEAVE READERS DESPERATE FOR MORE HAUNTING STORIES FROM THE SHOT IN THE DARK WORLD."
-SHEILA MASTERSON, AUTHOR OF THE LOST GOD SERIES

"IT DRAWS YOU IN, KEEPS YOU TETHERED, AND REFUSES TO LET GO... THE STORY OF EOIN AND ROISIN WILL LEAVE YOU BREATHLESS, TANGLED IN LONGING, FEAR, HEARTACHE, AND FLEETING JOY. "
-DARKACADEMIAREADS, GOODREADS

"HAUNTING, LYRICAL, AND UNSETTLING IN THE BEST WAY."
-JESSICA, GOODREADS

"I WAS UTTERLY CAPTIVATED—SPELLBOUND BY THE LYRICAL PROSE, ENTRANCED BY THE TENSION, AND COMPLETELY UNDONE BY THE DESCENT INTO MADNESS."
-NESSIA, GOODREADS

DEDICATION

To the SNL writer who first coined
'mark me down as scared and horny'...
we really took that to heart.

THREE YEARS EARLIER

EOIN

This winter will be the end of us all.

Last night's gathering in the chapel had been a miserable affair. I couldn't shake the memory of the wide eyes, the dismayed whispers.

This year's harvest isn't nearly enough.

Too many sheep have perished—we haven't enough wool.

We don't have enough fuel for the hearth.

The sickening echo of *not enough* kept me up through the night and prodded me into leaving my bed while the sky was still dark. Axe in hand, I set my sights on the distance and began walking.

Most of my kin wouldn't dare set foot in the forest before the sun had risen. In my grandmother's time, the stories of villagers falling prey to a banshee were so vicious that she only crossed the tree line when absolutely necessary.

As the primary craftsman of An Tulaigh, of course, I didn't have that luxury. Not anymore.

There was no shortage of stories from every cousin, friend, and visitor to our humble home. They wove tales of strange lights in the branches in the dead of night, special offerings begetting blessings and riches, and the cursed stones of Balleyboley.

I held one tale above all else as an absolute fact. The cold truth of it lived in my bones as my boots crunched along the fallen leaves that carpeted the ground. This forest was a sacred thing—the *thin space*. The place where the veil between our world and the fae's was shallow, making anything possible.

The sun, low on the horizon, turned the sky gray and cast strange shadows as I trekked onward, eyeing the moss-covered oaks. I hadn't gone far from the village path, yet the air thickened and surrounded me like a quiet embrace. It was hard not to feel watched—hard not to hear the echo of every frightening tale I'd heard as a child or over the dregs of midnight ales at festivals.

I was foolish to think I could finish cutting before the forest awoke. Standing within its shadows, I knew with coarse certainty that it never slept.

Get it over with. I stopped to survey.

Settling on a tree to strike was impossible when every option was surely punishable. Taking from the tree line could be misconstrued as an attempt to weaken the forest's boundaries, but choosing a tree from deeper within could be viewed as an outright attack.

The oaks around me were beautifully robust, entirely unlike the ones that had withered away near An Tulaigh. I swallowed hard at the prospect of returning home with wood for the hearth. I couldn't bear the thought of burying yet another body lost in the frigid night—and the full wrath of winter was still months away.

My fretful thoughts were silenced as my gaze was drawn to one of the oaks.

I swore a peculiar light was shining upon the rough bark. I stepped cautiously around the tangle of roots that plunged in and out of the earth around the tree. There was something different about this one. My ears rang with a hum that somehow sounded both near and distant.

Fae trickery.

And yet, I was transfixed. I raised my hand to touch the center of the trunk. As my fingers spread across the knotted texture, I released a sigh, feeling almost... *tranquil.*

A harsh rustle of vegetation snapped me from my lull. I automatically reached for my axe and staggered back in search of the source, only to catch my heel on a root and slash myself on the blade as I fell to the ground.

Brilliant pain burst along my forearm. Hissing, I pulled my arm in front of me. Blood trickled from the gash, traveling down my elbow and plopping onto the roots and leaves. Gritting my teeth, I held the wound against my cloak's fabric.

Quite brave, lad, I thought bitterly. *Startled by a rabbit in the bushes.*

But there was a charged sensation in the air—not unlike the tension before a lightning strike. I thought it was my own pulse in my ears, thrumming from the pain, but no. That was separate. Something else, carrying its own rhythm, occupied every conceivable space between the trees around me.

Holding my breath, I kept my eyes fixed on the wound, terrified of what I'd see when I looked up.

I had no choice.

Slowly, I lifted my gaze. At first, nothing seemed amiss.

And then, a hint of white behind the oak tree caught my eye. It was nearly invisible, easily mistaken for a trick of the light. But the longer I stared, the clearer it became: a ghostly pale hand gripped the trunk, the rest of its arm disappearing behind.

I eased backward and blinked hard, willing it to be nothing more than a frightened imagining. Tilting my head, I dared to seek a better look at the phantom owner of the hand that surely didn't exist.

The creature peeled away from the trunk and advanced toward me without a sound.

I found my footing at once and bolted. A scream caught in my throat. I refused to look back, certain the white hand would find my throat the second I dared.

Beware the banshees. The vengeful ghosts of the forest.

Such a creature couldn't be reasoned with. Though I had not yet taken anything from its home, my very presence here was an affront.

A moan escaped me as I realized the world was getting darker instead of lighter. I had fled deeper into the forest instead of away from it. I had no choice but to slow and watch my footing, desperate to outmaneuver the creature long enough to circle back in the direction of the village path.

"*You.*"

The voice came from in front of me.

I shouted when I looked up to find the creature directly in my path.

My footing stayed intact this time as I reached for my axe and held it in front of me in defense. A braver man—or stupider one—might have swung it immediately. But I steadied my breath and stared the creature head-on.

"I-I mean no harm," I stammered. "Stay back. Stay back and let me leave this place."

My words were silenced as I took a longer look at it—at *her*. Although the dawn was dark, she was stunningly visible, as though the moon itself shone from within her. The creature had the form of a woman teeming with unearthly beauty. Long white hair flowed down the length of her back. She wore a gown that seemed spun from the air itself.

"Let me leave," I breathed. "I won't return. Please—spare me. I meant no disrespect."

The woman tilted her head to the side, eyeing the axe. When her gaze traveled to meet mine, I couldn't breathe. She didn't appear frightened by the weapon nor moved by my plea. She stared at me with detached curiosity—animal-like and unsettling, like she hadn't decided what to do with me yet. She didn't seem to hold any particular emotion as she regarded me.

Perhaps she'll only attack if I strike, I thought with tentative hope.

Still clutching the axe, I attempted to step back in the direction I'd fled from.

From one blink to the next, she was directly before me. I didn't see her hand shoot out before it was grasping my arm. Her fingers dug into the still-bleeding wound.

"Release me!" I gasped, lurching back. Although she was a head shorter than I, the devastating strength of her grip kept me in place.

She leaned up while dragging me closer to her level until our faces were mere breaths apart. I was too frozen to fight. She looked up into my eyes, and the faintest flicker of... *something* stirred within those deep, dark pools.

Her voice, uncannily beautiful, surrounded me like a lover's touch. "You cannot hope to live if you take from the forest without blessing it. Take what you need. And nothing more."

A bout of dizziness swallowed me like a wave.

My eyelids fluttered madly, and all at once, I was surrounded by the soft light of dawn.

Staggering back, I drank in my environment, slack-jawed. Against all logic, I was back near the edge of the forest, as though I'd never left. The pain in my arm had vanished. I looked down in astonishment to find that the gash had completely closed, leaving no trace of a scar.

Breathing heavily, I searched in every direction for the strange, bewitching woman. Although I couldn't see her, I was almost certain that her gaze was currently resting upon me, observing my every movement.

My attention settled on the oak tree I had selected—and a pulse rang through my body, dissuading me from taking my axe to it. I selected another nearby and stepped up to it reverently.

A blessing.

I pressed my hand to the trunk and murmured. "I take not from you selfishly. I am indebted to your sacrifice." The words appeared on my lips as miraculously as the woman had appeared in front of me.

The first swing was the most frightening—but the woman was not toying with me. I was allowed to take what I could carry without punishment. All the while, I felt her watching.

The next trial—stepping out of the forest—was not met with any resistance, either. As my boots found the village path once again, I released a heavy breath and allowed my shoulders to relax. I had no intention of looking back, but something spurred me to do so.

Turning over my shoulder, I found two pinpricks of light hovering in the tall branches of the peculiar oak tree. Her eyes. As the faintest silhouette of her perched form became visible, I had a feeling I could only perceive her because she allowed it.

As I strode away, I couldn't shake the thought of what it might be like to touch her—to run my fingers through her moonlight hair or caress her soft skin.

I should bring her something next time.

A gift.

I

L ove was poison—and I was an abomination for allowing such primal stirrings to control me.

But what choice did I have? Countless men had passed through my forest. Hunters. Druids. Fools. They rushed and ravaged. They marched too loudly along the fallen leaves without care for the creatures sheltering nearby—but not *him*.

None were like my Eoin.

I couldn't remember how long I had been here. I had once tried to count the seasons, but they folded in on each other, harsh winters blurring into mild summers. Over and over. I knew I had been here a long time—perhaps centuries.

Lately, I wondered if I had been waiting for Eoin all this time.

From the forest, my sisters and I had watched his village grow. Where once a few simple cottages had been scattered around a central, hearty fire, dozens now sprawled over the land. Dwellings ranged from simple thatched-roof structures to manors in the hills that boasted fields of live-

stock. Further in the distance, a castle took form, harsh lines barely visible through the fog. The massive structure leeched more from the earth than the village itself.

As the humans' presence grew, the borders of the forest shrank. Yews, ash, and oak slowly vanished, like a festering wound. It took many decades—and a few brutal reminders—for balance to settle across the land.

Despite their ignorance and inclinations toward cruelty, humans were never short of activity: battles, celebrations, feasts, famine. Watching them from afar, I had always found myself torn between detached fascination and heartbreak. I could scarcely remember my time as one of them. It felt like someone else's distant dream. Flashes of rain on bare skin. Fingers in mine. Blood on moss. A gasp taken by the wind.

I was the forest now, or the forest was me. The lines blurred moment to moment.

Until *him*, nothing outside the forest had sparked joyful drumming in my chest.

And he would soon be here again.

The cool morning breeze curled through my unbound hair. I shut my eyes against the hazy glint of first light filtering through the trees and listened to the whisper of leaves all around. Ancient oaks groaned faintly, grass bowed, and the underbrush shifted as small creatures moved about in search of food.

Then, *footsteps*—the slow, steady rhythm of someone carefully plowing deeper into the woods.

I crawled higher on the wide, sloping oak branch, my bare feet digging in against the moss. The tree—*our tree*—stood as tall as the largest manor on the hill, providing me a bird's eye view of the ground below. I sensed Eoin before I saw him. His presence disrupted the birdsong and sent small animals fleeing to hide. The faint crunch of fallen leaves beneath his boots shattered the stillness, but he did not mean to cause commotion. His respect for my forest was reciprocated, and the trees seemed to bend around his presence, pleased.

A mop of tousled, ashy blond hair came into sight as Eoin tread into the grove of massive, moss-cloaked trees. I watched how he chose each step with such care, even as his weight sank into the earth the way my body never would. He had the lean, strong build that was common to craftsmen, with arms that pulled taut against the simple tunic tucked into his belted trousers. A half cloak was slung over his broad shoulders, protecting him against the early bite of autumn. The glint of his woodcutting axe was just visible beneath the folds of his cloak. The smell of him caught the air—woodsmoke and spice.

Each week without fail, his work brought him to the forest. He always remembered the proper blessings before he took his axe to my brothers, using their wood for his craft. Today, he carried something in his arms, covered in cloth and bound by twine. As I watched him take a seat beside the ribboning creek and turn his gaze patiently all around him, I was no longer content to watch from afar.

I descended to a lower branch and willed my form to be visible to mortal eyes—though he had likely sensed my stare by now, whether he could see me or not.

"What have you brought for me today?" I called down.

Eoin lifted his gaze, a smile brightening his stoic features as our gazes met. He held up the bundle, a challenge as much as it was an invitation.

"Come and see."

I dismounted, lowering myself down the centuries-old oak. His eyes flooded with gentle awe, as if he were watching silk itself unspool.

My bare feet hit the ground noiselessly. He straightened his shoulders at my approach—he always did, even though his fears that I was a vengeful *banshee* were long behind him. Years had passed, but it was as unsettling as it was beautiful for him to see how the earth responded to me. As I approached, the grass straightened, the water's gurgle brightened. Primrose and clover unfurled along my path, quiet as a whisper.

"Show me," I demanded, beaming as I dropped beside him on the mossy earth. I placed my hands on his thigh with an impatient tug. "Have you crafted another gift?"

Eoin smiled, his eyes tracing the wild, silvery locks that hung over my shoulders. "How could I resist?"

He offered the package to me. I gave a chirrup of delight as I tore off the twine and unwound the cloth, revealing a rectangle of ash wood with a female figure carved into its surface. Garlands of primroses and ivy were sculpted around her like a frame. I traced my fingertips over the woodwork, where a faint etching of a face stared back at me.

"It's you, little niamh." Eoin's arm settled around my waist, pulling me into his side. He inspected his handiwork proudly. "What do you think? Have I captured your beauty?"

"Quite an impossible feat for mortal hands," I answered. "But a *very* good attempt. Thank you." I clutched the piece to my chest, gifting him a wide smile. The thought of him toiling away by the fire's light, etching my likeness with delicate strokes... I nearly purred at the flattery.

"And for me?" Eoin had grown delightfully bold in the last few months. He put his hand over mine, lifting his brow. "Have you brought me riddles or treasures today?"

My hand looked as weightless as a child's compared to his—larger and calloused, shaped by years of labor. He was warm and coarse and *alive,* so unlike the marble sheen of my complexion. Though his touch had become familiar, the juxtaposition made my heart drum.

He was everything I was not, and where my sisters might find disgust in the contrast, I found delight. Flecks of greed entered his gaze when he looked at me sometimes, and I treasured that, too. He prided himself on being the only villager with such a *secret* waiting for him deep in the woods. His little niamh.

Day by day, I found I did not mind the concept—belonging to him.

"I do have something for you," I said. "I will give you a tear."

Eoin's eyebrows pulled together. "A tear?"

I nodded, letting the woodwork rest in my lap so I might pluck at the base of his throat, where the glorious thrum of his pulse hummed, quickening. "If you accept it, you'll not age a day," I told him. "You'll never grow ill, never bear weathered skin."

My touch strayed to his cheek. He recoiled as though my soft skin had burned him. Shadows crossed over his handsome face, giving me pause.

"Keep your tear, little niamh. I would never want to make you weep," he said, offering a shaky laugh.

Such compassion. So kind, my Eoin. But I knew fear when I heard it.

Fear was simply the natural order for humans when it came to entities far beyond their understanding. Fear meant power, meant respect.

Why did it wither me to hear it from him?

"I've thought of another gift, then," I pressed, intent on deterring him from taking his leave. "You may give me a name."

Again, Eoin's eyebrows lifted—but this time, his smirk returned. "After these years, why now?"

His fingers were heavier on my waist.

I shot him a feline smile. "Do you want it or not?"

"Give me a moment! Let me think," Eoin chuckled.

His gaze went distant with thought. For a moment, the bright gurgle of the creek was all that could be heard throughout the clearing. I relished the pause—every moment of musing prolonged our time together.

"I think I'll call you...*Róisín*," Eoin said at last, giving me an all-too stoic stare—the one that masked a playful glitter behind his eyes.

A shiver of pleasure raced through me.

"Róisín," I murmured, feigning uncertainty. *Little Rose.*

He watched me with careful reverence, awaiting my approval. The name hung in the air between us, and I had no reason to dwell in its silent echo, but I couldn't deny myself the delight of watching him squirm. My smile was carefully subdued. "It is acceptable."

His lips parted, and he appeared to wrestle between relief and disappointment before settling on the latter. "*Acceptable?* I dare you to find a name that suits you more."

He'd grown bold, my human. I recalled a time when he wouldn't have dreamed of voicing disagreement with me. The name he'd chosen was perfect—absolutely *perfect*—but my mask refused to slip and reveal the blessing he'd given me. None of my sisters had names. We had no need for such mortal trifles, not when we were all pieces of the same forest. Fragments of one divine being.

But I was different. *He* had made me different, and with each visit, whether he knew it or not, he coaxed me further from my true nature.

My smile sharpened into a grin. "Come now, I've given you a marvelous gift, allowing you to name me. To change it now would be unfair."

His eyes met mine, searching. When his features relaxed, I wondered if he'd seen through my facade and found the elation buried beneath. "Róisín," he said firmly, leaning closer. "I can think of no greater gift, my little rose."

The ground shivered beneath us. Eoin drew back, scanning the forest floor with wide-eyed wonder until he found the source of the commotion directly beside us: branches sprouted from the earth, climbing and thickening until the tops were level with his chest. Vibrant leaves burst out in clusters first, followed by roses of the deepest red—dozens from bud to blossom in a matter of seconds.

"You are a marvel," Eoin said with untethered wonder as he reached for one of the blooms.

He hissed upon contact and flinched, leaving the rose. A wet touch of red marred the tip of the thorn that had bitten him. At once, a ravenous sensation flamed through me, and I only had eyes for the fresh bead of crimson dotting the base of his finger.

I leaned across him to take his hand tenderly in mine. "Allow me," I said. I kissed the wound, tracing the tip of my tongue over the dewdrop of blood, savoring its taste.

"You're too kind," he murmured as the wound closed beneath my affection. I suppressed a shiver, desperate for more, *more*, but I couldn't bear the thought of frightening him away. Not my Eoin. I released his hand.

"I suppose I should apologize for that," I said, peering at the wickedly sharp thorns of the rose bush. "But the forest must protect itself, after all. What good is a plucked rose?"

He chuckled. "Don't be so cynical. A cut rose is the sort of gift that makes my people happy."

Sniffing, I shook my head. "A gift which withers for the sake of momentary wonder. How very mortal of you." My hand floated up to trace his jawline with my fingertips. I stared hard into his eyes. "You sound far too familiar with the notion. Don't tell me you're offering such gifts to others?"

That hint of caution returned, hardening in the dawn light flecking across his face. He caught my hand and brought it to his lips, kissing my knuckles tenderly. "I have little time for such things when I'm so busy perfecting *your* gifts, my little rose. Speaking of—" Eoin released my hand to scoop up the engraved panel resting in my lap. He skimmed his handiwork with a proud gleam in his eyes before looking back at me. "Where shall you place this one?"

I squeezed his leg. "Perhaps you can help me decide."

I rose to my feet, dancing from one mossy stone to the next. My steps were weightless, my ivory skirts swirling like ripples of water around my legs with every nimble stride.

"Slow down!" Eoin barked, having barely risen to his feet in the time I was halfway across the brook. "Don't leave me in your shadow again. I swear I heard a Formorian last time."

He followed me, trodding on the mossy rocks that jutted over the shallow water. Several steps had to be recalculated, as he was too cumbersome to use the same slivers of stone that I could balance on. When he was nearly to the bank, he chose a weak formation for his next step. The rock snapped, half crumbling into the water, leaving Eoin windmilling for balance with the wooden etching still clutched protectively in his grasp.

I leaned out and caught his free hand in mine, clasping firmly. *I won't lose you,* I thought, smiling up at him. Something softened in his expression, like he understood me. Even if he had the human inclination to fear the forest and its obstacles, perhaps I was slowly awakening *his* true nature as much as he was awakening mine.

Surprise mingled with the relief in Eoin's face—hesitant to lean his full weight against me, as though it might hurt me. His grip strengthened, and I hauled him to the bank beside me.

With his strong fingers still wound through mine, I led him onward, deeper into my home.

2

"**Y**ou're afraid."

Eoin's trepidation was understandable, though it made me prickle nonetheless. His work as a craftsman didn't require him to source materials this far from the village, and I rarely guided him so far from our special tree.

What was it about *today* that made me pull him toward the most towering oaks, where shadows cast darkness like fingers of night?

His jaw was set. "I'm not."

His pulse whispered against my skin where our hands were still joined. A part of me was thrilled at it as I tugged him forward. His lack of resistance was promising, although uncertain.

"Your heart is hammering. You're afraid of the forest, but I *am* the forest. You can see why it wounds me." I squeezed his hand, craning my neck to steal his gaze, to set him at ease. "I've told you before—you are a welcome guest here."

"Tolerated, more like." Eoin's sharp attention drifted from tree to tree, reverent of the invisible eyes of my sisters.

I bit my lip, burying a coy smile at the swirling whispers he couldn't hear. It was true, though I'd loathe to admit it to him; while my sisters loved me ardently, they did not see the appeal of becoming so familiar with a mortal. Dirty, fragile, clumsy.

And *brief*. Most villagers did not see past their forty-fifth birthday.

I glanced at Eoin's profile, still in the prime of his life.

But a lifetime to him was a mere moment for me.

When I thought of Eoin withering away and set into that formidable, monolithic tomb where all the other villagers from generations were laid to rest...

Ice crept through my body. Fear and anger writhed in my chest. My very soul howled at the abomination of it. Such an ending did not befit someone like him.

"Little niamh?" Eoin stopped short, wheeling me to face him. "Róisín? What's wrong?"

My vision of him was clouded for a moment. When I surfaced, I blinked at the startling clarity of his face hovering over mine. Still alive. Still mine. Then—

"Oh, I'm sorry," I stammered.

Around us, a web of blackened brambles had burst from the ground. To my alarm, they were deformed from their natural growth, curling into agonized shapes that stretched outward, climbing over each other rather than aspiring toward sunlight.

I could hardly believe I was capable of producing such a thing after the rose bush.

Eyes wide, I took a steadying breath and comforted the earth. The forest seemed to exhale in time with me. Crackling surrounded us as the brambles flattened to the ground. The thorns fell from the vines in a soft clatter. Soon, the tangle was reduced to a peculiar carpet around us. Peculiar, but harmless.

"I am the forest," I offered in a weak breath.

Eoin's brow knitted, glancing from me to the growth encircling us. Despite being unsettled, he offered the kindness of tucking silvery hair behind my ear and tipping my face up to examine me.

"What could possibly prey on that beautiful mind of yours?"

The gesture shouldn't have felt as delightful as it did. My sisters whispered in the branches like an ornery gust of wind. I turned from him, ushering him behind me. "We're nearly at the spot."

I had chosen this grove with care. A human would have never found such a verdant location on their own. Here, the trees twisted higher and spread further; the grass was softer, the flowers brighter. A crystal-clear pond lay at the center, fed by a spring that pulsed beneath the earth like a heartbeat.

The steady thud of his boots paused behind me. He searched his surroundings with reverent intimidation before meeting my questioning gaze.

"I may not be afraid, but it doesn't feel proper for me to be here," he admitted in a hushed voice. "This place—it feels strange. It's for those like *you*."

Always observant. He didn't plow through the world like other humans I'd encountered. No, he watched. He reflected.

"You are safe and welcome," I said resolutely. "So long as you are with me, you belong." I returned to him with soundless steps until I was tilting my head back to hold his eyes. I slipped my fingers into his. "Do you believe me?"

His lips parted, his honeyed eyes flickering over me. "You've yet to lead me astray, little niamh. If I am here, then I trust you."

My heart swelled. I wanted to lean closer, to press my cheek to his chest and bask in the warmth of his pulse, but he looked past me and tensed suddenly. Following his gaze, I found a small family of deer entering the grove—a doe with twin fawns. The creatures regarded us for only a moment before proceeding toward the pond.

"Come," I whispered, tugging Eoin in the direction of the deer.

"I'll frighten them."

"You're no hunter," I said, throwing a teasing grin over my shoulder.

The deer did not flee upon our approach—on the contrary, the fawns trotted closer curiously. The mother bowed her head in deference to me before returning to her tranquil drink from the pond. I extended a hand, stroking the soft head of the nearest fawn, only to have the other bleat and stamp its hooves in protest for attention.

Eoin chuckled, tentatively mirroring my action. The second fawn regarded him with suspicious stillness before ducking its head under his palm, unafraid. The soft wonder on his face made my breath catch.

"Incredible," he murmured, smiling at me as though I'd given him another gift.

The fawns were not content to stay still for long. One backed up and shook its head playfully, and the other followed suit. The two of them bounded off together around the pond, chasing one way and then hopping in the other direction.

"I've never seen such carefree creatures," Eoin said.

"They know they are safe here."

The doe calmly lifted her head from the pond and exited the grove, her fawns circling her as their game continued, unbroken. For a few long moments after they disappeared, Eoin still stared after them.

I approached the pond, kneeling to slip my hand under the water. Eoin sensed my stare upon him. Not breaking his gaze, I took hold of the hem of my dress, wading into the water. It lapped against me like a kiss of coolness, plastering the lighter-than-air fabric of my gown against my ankles. The pond was deep at its center, with water so pure you could see right to the bottom where tiny tench fish darted between moss-covered rocks.

"Come and dance with me," I called out, whirling back to face him.

"In there?" Eoin barked a laugh. "I'll freeze, are you mad?"

My smile turned wicked. "You're as cautious as a child."

After a moment of hesitation, he submitted to my coaxing and knelt by the bank to slip his hand into the water. He tensed at the sensation, then relaxed. The bewilderment on his face was charming—his wonderment seemed in unlimited supply during our times together.

"See? It's perfectly warm," I said. And it would remain that way, so long as he stayed by my side.

Stepping before him, I unfastened his cloak, biting back a grimace at the slight sting of the iron clasp against my skin. My forwardness earned an alarmed look, but his gaze then fell longingly to the water, glittering with refractions of dawn's first rays. He dragged a hand over his face, grinning and shaking his head.

"Well, I will not stand here and be called a child." Eoin set aside the wooden carving to tear off his boots and tunic, much to my delight.

I backed away as he waded into the pond, my heart pounding with a wild glee. Eoin chased me, catching me around the waist and making me squeal with laughter. I wriggled and kicked with threats that were as potent as wet paper until he at last set me back on my feet, his mirth buried into my neck. I turned, finding him submerged to his waist, and rivets of water running down his toned arms and chest. I was delightfully aware of how his eyes drifted downward, the delicate fabric of my gown all but disappearing as the water lapped just below my breasts.

Birdsong and rustling leaves gathered in the silence, surrounding us better than any musicians. I danced, shutting my eyes and throwing up my arms, swirling my heavy skirts in the deep water. There was always music in the woods, for anyone careful enough to hear it.

"Don't humans dance?" I asked, drifting closer to him.

As he watched me dance—the way my sisters and I always did, joyously and untethered—something gave in Eoin's polite mannerisms. In perhaps his boldest act since meeting me years ago, he put his arms out and intercepted me.

"Not like that," he said, positioning me.

When I looked up at his face, I swore I could melt into his golden-brown eyes. I'd certainly die if he ever looked at anyone else with such smoldering tenderness.

Our breathing fell into sync, the two of us finding a new, playful dance. He lifted his arm and twirled me, grinning as I let my body sink into our invisible rhythm at his lead. Peace settled into my heart like never before. I might have held onto him forever if he hadn't interrupted the sounds of the forest.

"If only I could smuggle you into the village, my little rose. I could show the same hospitality that you have so offered me," Eoin murmured, his voice a gentle rumble like earth shifting.

"It's not a matter of hospitality on your part. I cannot leave the forest." I reached up to trace his jaw with my fingertips. "You must understand, then, why my sisters and I are so protective of our home. It is ours by right, and all we have. Humans stake claims wherever they travel, while creatures of the forest cannot stray far."

Eoin frowned. "What would happen to you? If you stepped out of these woods, I mean."

I dropped my gaze to our hands, still clasped. Two worlds intertwined. "I am the forest. Less than a day away from it could drain everything I am," I offered in a low voice. "It would be painful, to say the least."

"I'm sorry," Eoin murmured.

"Don't be. There is more joy here than I could ever find out there."

The disappointment in his gaze weighed heavily upon my heart as he leaned down, resting his forehead against mine. The gentle smile in his voice, however, alleviated the pain. "I suppose you'll have to remain my little secret, then."

His.

The displeased murmurs of my sisters had never felt further away. Didn't they understand that logic could never hope to compete with infatuation?

We were so close. All I needed to do was tip my mouth a bit higher to catch his lips.

Patience. I had to be patient.

I forced a passive expression on my face and waded backward, putting inches between us that felt like a gaping canyon.

As I clambered back onto the bank, I grasped the wooden carving from beside Eoin's discarded clothing. "Have you forgotten why we're here?" I asked, raising my eyebrows. "Where shall we put it?"

Eoin waded back, giving a little shiver as he stepped back into the cool morning air beside me. "It is your gift, Róisín. You should decide."

My answer arrived with an insulted little scoff. "I'll do no such thing! Why have I brought you here if not for your artistic eye?"

"Why indeed," Eoin murmured. I saw how his searching gaze caught on one of the tree hollows overhead.

"That's a fine spot," I prompted before he could point it out himself.

"Ah, it's too high up. No footholds," he said, gesturing at the thick column of the trunk. The soft moss clinging to the rivets would do him no favors, but my form held none of the clumsy boundaries of a mortal.

I savored the weight of his astounded gaze as I scaled the tree with the ease of something feline. My movements were unhurried—I sensed how his stare traced every curve of my body through my gown, still translucent and dripping cool water.

After delicately placing his gift in the hollow, I admired him from above. Even from a distance, I noted how he held his breath, worried about my precarious perch yet wanting nothing more to continue gazing upon me.

After descending with the same ease, I took his hand and led him to sit at the edge of the pond. Seated in the soft grass side by side, I gazed up at the carving he'd made of me. My own miniature likeness stared back.

"Do you see?" I said. "It fits perfectly. Taken from the forest, returned to the forest. All is as it should be."

Water trickled down his shoulders and chest. He sighed, turning to me with wonder in his stare. "The way you view the world is...so unlike anyone else I've met." He drew his fingers through a lock of my damp hair, searching my face. "I'm honored to have earned your company, Róisín."

My breath stammered, and I sat with the strangeness of it, once again reminded that I had never felt such stirrings before *him*. Touching was simply touching—it didn't have to *mean* anything more. At least, that used to ring true. But now...

My gaze turned downward to the clear pool of water before us. Our reflections sat close together, and though

I longed to sink into the delight of the view, I inhaled sharply.

"What's wrong?" Eoin asked, drawing my eyes back to his.

"I—" Glancing at our reflection once more, I confirmed what I knew to be true. "Is that really what I look like?"

Bewildered, he glanced between me and my reflection as though he expected to find one different from the other. "What do you mean? You look like you belong in the halls of the castle. I doubt even that does you justice—you look higher than royalty." He searched me once more and leaned in closer. "You're like a beautiful dream. A *goddess*."

He said it in a whisper, as though he very well may speak his assessment into truth.

Clenching my jaw, I glared between the trees, toward distant hills. The castle was barely a smudge on the horizon behind a shroud of mist. He followed my gaze, and I was all too aware of how he grew tense beside me.

I didn't want to be merely a dream.

"Have I offended you?" he asked.

"You amended your statement well," I said airily, sneering at the faraway structure. "Mortals who live in castles think too highly of themselves." My gaze softened upon him. "You shouldn't aspire to such things. You're worth a dozen of them."

The tension in his shoulders eased, his gaze turning wistful. "Believe me, I'm content with the simple life I've built for myself in An Tulaigh, but...I cannot deny that I'm curious about what it must be like over there. Imagine it—having servants, feasts every night, a stable packed with horses to take you as far as the eye can see."

My attention fell back to my reflection—and Eoin hadn't rambled for long before he noticed.

"What troubles you about your appearance?" he asked.

"I look *different* since I last regarded myself," I insisted. Less of the forest. More mortal. The thought sent a roil of disgust through me, but then again, I would never call my dear Eoin disgusting.

He frowned. "You *are* different," he agreed. "You've changed. I've only glimpsed others of your kind—your siblings, as you say. A mere glint of spark-like eyes at dusk. It's little wonder the frightful legends in my village have yet to cease. Stories of illusions, poisoned gifts, and wanderers walking until they collapsed."

I stared impassively. If he knew the things I had done over the centuries, he would certainly look upon me differently. There was a time when I wouldn't have cared.

"But I find it harder these days to believe you're of kin with the others," he finished. "Why?"

You, I thought fiercely. *You have made me this way.*

From the moment he bled on my roots on the day we met years ago, he had changed me. And with each visit, he only furthered the transformation. I held my tongue at the thought of telling him. Would it frighten his simple mortal mind to know how involved he was in awakening me to this world of consuming emotions?

Would our bond frighten him away?

No, I couldn't tell him.

Stay, the forest whispered around us, echoing my desperate desires for him. *Stay forever. Stay—*

I raised my eyebrows haughtily. "Is every mortal the same?" I questioned back. "*You* are different from your kind, too, you strange creature. No others are so bold as to venture so far into the forest these days."

Eoin traced the side of my face with his fingertips. His deep voice softened. "If every mortal were so bold, I wouldn't have you all to myself, now would I, little niamh?"

Shivering, I considered how easily I could keep him forever. To make him stay. But the iron claws of sorrow latched onto my heart at the thought of forcing him. These years with his company truly had softened me.

I wanted—no, *needed*—him to choose me without resorting to the tricks his kind feared so deeply. He was different, my Eoin.

And if he didn't come willingly, I couldn't keep him.

Our faces were so close that I felt his breath unfurl against my cheek. His hand, large and calloused, still cradled my head with care unbefitting a woodsman. That gleam in his eyes—it was molten and greedy and *real*.

Closing what little space remained between us, I wound my arms around him and pressed my lips to his.

3

E oin made a small noise at the back of his throat—surprise, then pleasure.

The forest hummed in harmony, pulsing in time with my heart. The warmth of his lips cut through the autumn chill, making me feel as though the most brilliant light was glowing within me.

As my arms tightened around him, he deepened our kiss. His hands settled around my waist, drawing me firmly against him.

This was *right*.

Mine, I thought. *All mine.*

But far too soon, he startled and let me go. Frowning, I tried to lean up for another kiss, only to have him grasp my shoulders to keep me at arm's length.

"It's—that's—" Eoin sputtered. His voice was caught in a breathless register, his eyes wild. "We shouldn't have done that."

"Why?" I traced his knuckles, letting a soft smile curve my lips. "Didn't you enjoy it?"

A flush was rising into his face, and the shock began to melt into confusion. His brown eyes skated over my expression in an attempt to read me. I wished he *would* for a moment—I wished Eoin could see straight through my passive mask to the sweet agony burdened inside me.

"I've daydreamed about it," he admitted, words choking out like a sinful confession. He released me and raked a hand through his damp hair. "For years. But I never imagined *actually*—" He blinked hard, eyes beginning to go distant. "I don't even know what you really are."

"But you know *who* I am," I reminded him. "You've said it yourself."

With my fingers soft against his cheek, I guided him gently downward.

"Come here," I murmured.

He resisted for a moment, unsure of himself—unsure of me. But something in him yielded, allowing me to draw him down and cradle his head in my lap, like it was the most natural thing in the world. Like we weren't divided by everything we were.

For a moment, I allowed myself to believe it.

I threaded my fingers into his golden-brown hair, slow and steady. Eoin's eyes fluttered, growing heavy. Those long lashes flickered gold in the early sunlight. I hummed a song for him—just for him. Something ancient, something quiet. His breathing slowed, his doubt unfurling like wind against water.

The weight of his body against mine was everything I craved. Couldn't he feel it too? How we were something rare and wild and wonderful?

"No one else knows." My voice was soft as silk. "You've done nothing wrong."

Tension rippled through his shoulders. His words were a low rumble. "I don't know what it means. What *you* mean."

I leaned over him, my pale hair falling like a veil between us and the forest. "Don't let your humanity preclude you from simple pleasures," I whispered with an impish smile.

Eoin must've sensed my smile—he cracked a small grin, too. A small, unconscious moan slipped from his throat as I worked my fingers through his hair.

Although the sun would soon signal the new day, his eyelids fell halfway, a languid sigh streaming through his parted lips—all thoughts of his duties rinsed from his mind. So relaxed. So at home.

Stay with me, I thought. *You are happy here.*

Stay, the forest echoed. *Stay, stay.*

It was the pulse of a heartbeat growing stronger. Vibrant flowers and fresh ferns bloomed through the grove. *Stay.* A home pulsing with life that would never fade, never die. *Stay, stay.*

"A niamh's tear is a precious gift," I murmured, leaning closer to him. "A pure gift. One that requires nothing in return. You can feel like this forever."

For a moment, Eoin relaxed further as though he might fall asleep. But his eyes snapped open and widened. He sat up suddenly, gasping for breath. He gave me an odd, tense look before composing himself with visible care.

I remembered with a sinking heart that he was a man who had been told too many frightening myths about this place. About *me*.

"The sun is rising," he said, each word clipped and breathless. He raked his gaze around us, settling on his discarded clothes and axe. "I should go. The day's nearly upon us. Someone will come looking for me if I don't return soon."

The day. As though our time together were nothing but a dream in the wee hours of the morning. Would I only have him while he was entranced? Never a full life. Never real.

A spark of wrath roared through my chest, and I had the sudden urge to abandon him in the grove—simply melt into the foliage. If he truly held the rarity that I fawned over, then he could wander the forest until he was part of it—until he was begging for me to save him, voice ragged and echoing through the woods.

It would be easy to forget him for a few days, I thought cruelly.

But I couldn't do that. Not to my Eoin.

Early golden light painted the sculpted muscles of his back as he bent to gather his things. He dressed, tucking his tunic into his still-wet trousers. I supposed he would simply explain *that* away by claiming he took a fall into the creek. Erasing me yet again.

While Eoin was still fastening his cloak around his shoulders, I picked up his axe, weighing it in my hands. Its worn iron blade glared up at me in silent threat. I angled the heavy tool a little further from my body, all too happy to pass it into Eoin's grasp.

My smile was as passive as a doe's as I took his free hand and led him back the way we had traveled. When the towering oaks became sparser and more sunlight penetrated the canopy, he wheeled us to a stop and took care in selecting his tree.

"What is it you're tasked with making this time?" I asked.

"Bedframes." Eoin circled a modest birch, its trunk not much larger than his forearm. "More mouths to house and feed every day, it seems."

He ran his hands over the bark, tipping his head back to survey the tangle of leaves that vanished toward the heavens. My breath caught when his hands brushed over the bark—I felt the caress of his calloused palms over the small of my back. I swore I could sense the heat of his touch.

Could he see the grass at his feet stretching upward, yearning to reach him while I held my breath to keep from sighing?

Eoin turned over his shoulder, scrutinizing me with a shadowed look on his face. "You're sure it doesn't hurt you when I do this?"

"I feel it," I said. "But the forest is too vast and strong for me to call it pain. You have my permission."

Eoin nodded reverently before kneeling at the tree's base, reciting a blessing over it. My sisters appeared in my peripheral—nearly twelve of them, their pale faces stoic. They perched in branches and peered around the sides of oaks, watching with their silent, piercing opal eyes. I was not particularly surprised to see them crowding us, drawn by his blessing and the sharp tang of iron. We always came to mourn the loss of one of our brothers.

Eoin rose to his feet, unaware of the many eyes on him as he raised his axe and swung hard. We all flinched together as the axe swung down again, *again*. It was seven impacts before the birch surrendered and fell. He moved with the practiced ease of someone who had done this a hundred times, and I tempered my expression in front of my sisters—if not for myself, then to not give away to Eoin how many eyes were truly upon him as he labored.

Eventually, I too let myself vanish from his sight. He chopped the wood into workable pieces, loading as much as he could carry in his arms for the first journey. He turned to say farewell, only to find I had melted into the forest—standing right before him, yet invisible to mortal eyes.

"Goodbye, Róisín," he whispered, the ghost of a smile on his lips.

The sun was full overhead, basking in a blanket of scattered grey clouds. I followed him to the edge of the forest, guarding him from the wolves that eyed him hungrily, the stinging nettle that rose toward his heels. I was the shadow he could not see, the wind at his back.

When his boots hit cobblestone instead of packed earth, I hit resistance. The hum of energy deepened as I raised my hands toward the very edge of the forest. My ears rang with the silent warning.

Go no further.

Rocking back on my heels in the dirt, I watched Eoin until he vanished from sight, another figure in the maze of houses, taverns, and stables.

Soon, I thought. *Soon he will choose me.*

Soon, the forest whispered, blossoming around me with the excitement of accepting a new denizen.

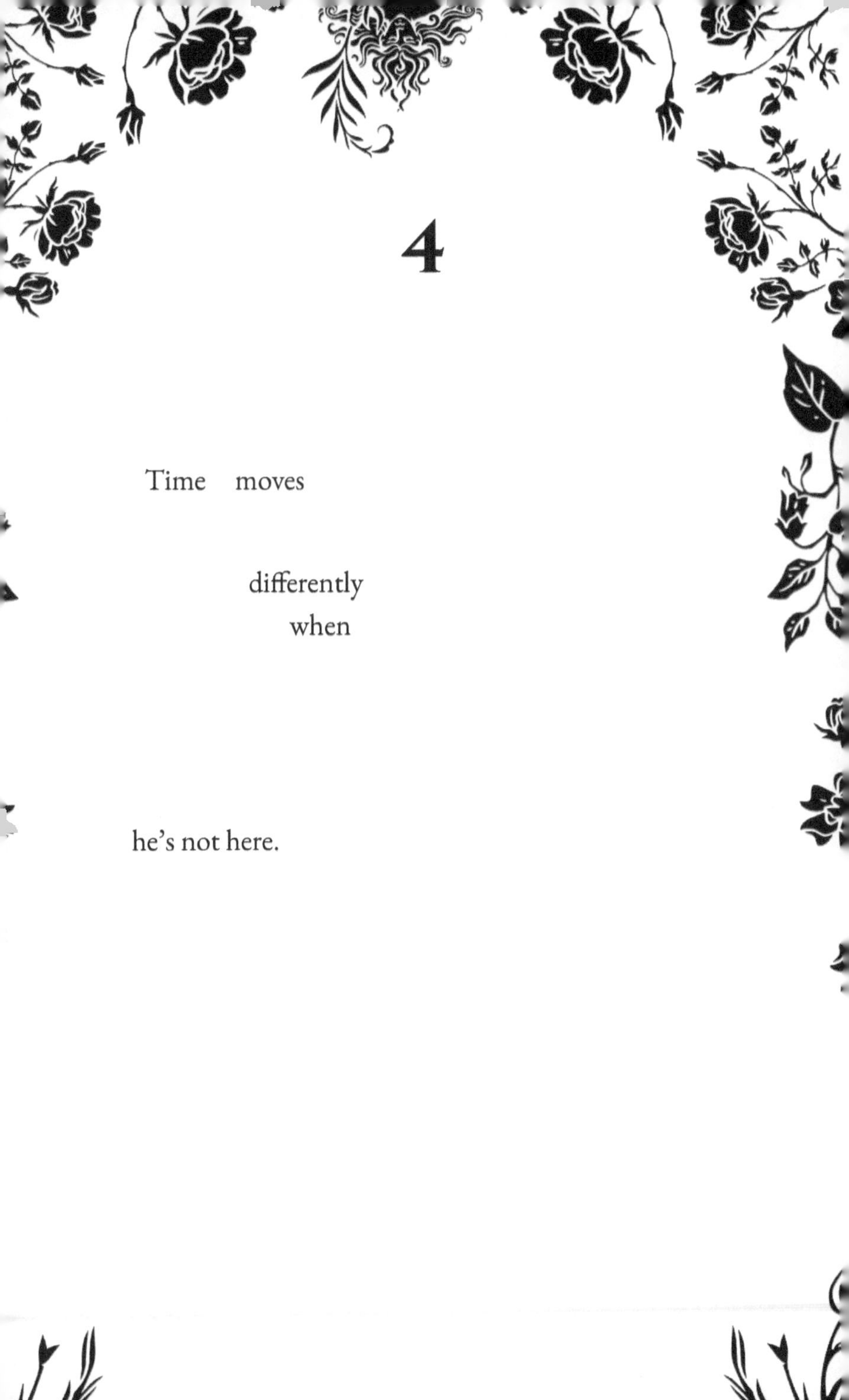

4

Time   moves

differently
when

he's not here.

5

The air turned crisp as days unraveled into weeks. I thought my kiss would have been enough to send Eoin carving a hundred wooden portraits of my countenance, to spellbind his very soul.

I'd seen far less do much more to a man.

Instead, something else seemed to prey on his mind. His visits became less frequent as autumn marched on. He was distracted, even when I showed him more marvels of the forest—blossoming sweet summer berries that burst like sweets on his tongue, the oldest oak draped in rich moss, roses that glittered with dew from dawn until dusk.

He still called me his *little Róisín*—but none of it could inspire wonder in him the way it used to. His gifts, too, became lackluster—commonplace carvings with more simplistic strokes than I knew Eoin's talented hands were capable of.

I made my gifts more extravagant to excite him: healing salves, a rose that would never die or lose its sweet scent. I pressed handfuls of seeds that would yield more food, even

in the harshest winter. He accepted all of these with smiles devoid of the worship I longed to see reflected at me.

Dance with us, my sisters whispered. They were the rustle of the wind, the groaning of crooked branches swaying, the chirp of goldcrests. How could I dance or tend to meadows when this wrongness gnawed at my chest, a hollow sensation my kind were never meant to bear?

Day after day, I refused them. My sisters' faces, so similar to my own, reflected pity. Was it so terrible to give in to this yearning?

Days became weeks, and Eoin neglected our morning visits time and again. Still, I stayed rooted in my favorite tree overlooking the clearing, watching for him. Waiting.

Was he growing tired of me?

Impossible. That was impossible.

Every time he left, Eoin gazed over his shoulder at me as though it pained him to pull his eyes from me. He had *named me.*

Perhaps it was worse than that.

As winter wove itself through the forest, I feared the very worst had come to pass—that I had not saved him soon enough from his mortal fate. The cold was harsh. Frost choked my brother trees, rendering their lush branches barren and dark. The very thought made me want to sink beneath the earth. Down and down, never to emerge.

The forest around me, usually so resilient to the cold, gave in to winter's bite at the tree line, where I spent my days waiting. My sisters ceased calling to me, unable to bear entering the ground I had poisoned in my sorrow. Perhaps when spring came around, this spot would stay rotten for centuries to come.

But Eoin did return.

At first, I thought he was no more than a dream or a different mortal, but no. It was *him*.

My Eoin was in the clearing, approaching the forest, his steps light despite the layer of snow and the frigid air.

I wasted no time on games. I did not hide, did not wait to reveal myself at the opportune moment to startle him. I moved to the edge of the trees. My steps halted of their own accord because I was the forest and the forest was me.

Leaning heavily against a tree trunk, I caught my breath. Even now, fresh life began through the tree, its happiness spreading to the roots of others now that Eoin had finally returned, alive and well.

"Róisín?" Eoin paused when he saw me before hurrying forward. "Are you alright?"

The moment he was within reach, I sank against him. Strong arms supported me, warmer than anything I had touched in weeks. He dropped to his knees, lowering me gently and holding me against him. I wound my arms around him and pressed the side of my face into his chest fervently. His heartbeat was hammering a delicious *thump, thump, thump*. I could have listened for hours.

He was here. He was real. I could not bear to put on the pretense of disinterest, and all my bitterness lay buried beneath a sense of relief I had never once experienced.

"I thought you'd died!" I whispered with fierce sorrow.

He tensed in surprise, then held me tighter.

"My little niamh," he murmured. "I'm sorry. I'm so, so sorry. The days slipped by me. Preparing for winter kept me busy, and provisions were low."

"I gave you the seeds!" I pulled away to look him full in the face, some anger winning out. "Their harvest will persevere through the harshest storm—I told you!" He didn't sound nearly sorry enough. He should have known I'd have worried. Should have known I was not a trifle to be ignored.

He smiled tenderly. "I know—and what a great help those seeds were. I can never repay you enough. But travelers have settled into the village over the weeks, and I have been needed for construction—nothing that upsets the boundaries of your forest, of course."

My elation wavered, a lone flower amid a storm. He seemed so...*happy*. But it was a distracted sort of happiness, one that he had been carrying for some time, long before he decided to finally show his face in my forest. I clasped my hand around his wrist and did not blink.

"There is more," I said. "Tell me why else you haven't been to visit."

Sighing, he broke away from my stare, though that far-away smile remained at the corners of his lips. "I have good news—brilliant news, really. I...I am engaged. One of the travelers who settled—she is to be my wife."

I went very still, staring at him as he pressed on, his enthusiasm building with each word. Eoin took my silence as a keen invitation, describing his betrothed. His voice bubbled with warmth, but to my ears, it was like dissonant strings—grating me as he described her beauty, her kindness, her effortless charm.

Eoin's warm arms around me felt feverish now, stifling.

Faint crackling sounded around us—brambles darkening and whitebeam trees shivering with my contempt.

Control. I could not afford to frighten him again.

Chest tight with shallow breaths, I leaned away from Eoin to put space between our faces, and balled my fists in my gown. I squeezed so hard that my nails dug painfully into my palms. If blood still ran through my veins, scarlet crescents would have marred my skin. The forest eased like a breeze settling.

"You would love her as I do, I'm sure of it," Eoin said, his boyish grin still bright in the pale wintery sun. "She's no stranger to venturing into the wilds of our strange country. She has an adventurous spirit, like that of any fox." Eoin's large, calloused hand slipped around both of mine and squeezed meaningfully. "I'd like to bring Brianna here to see the forest in all its glory. To see *you.*"

What a hideous name.

"No." The word flew from my lips without a thought.

Eoin's grin froze like he didn't quite believe me, a furrow pulling between his eyes. Silence crackled between us. A frozen wind cut through the clearing—one that I could not quite feel, yet made an instinctive shiver race through Eoin despite the heavy cloak he donned.

"No? But—why?" he asked. "You don't need to be frightened of her."

His hand squeezed mine again—a beacon of heat. That seductive pulse of his hammering against my frigid skin.

"I'm not scared of that woman," I snarled. "I fear no mortal."

His gaze dropped, darkness clouding his features. "Perhaps you should. Sometimes I worry for you. The Wild Hunt has been on the move. Tales spread of their victories over a village of changelings, and the Aos Sídhe of Ulaid." His eyes lifted, pinning me with their sudden intensity. "It sickens me to imagine the Hunt coming here. What they might do to you."

Memories stirred—torches and wicked metals. Screaming, though I could not distinguish my own voice from my sisters'. Though it had been decades ago, the memory remained like a dark smudge—impossible to clear away, no matter how many years passed.

Though I didn't need Eoin's protection, my heart squeezed at the thought of what he would do for me.

"The last hunters who tried to harm my forest now lie beneath it," I told him.

Eoin swallowed, his gaze scanning my face. "Brianna isn't like those brutes. You should have seen her face when I showed her your rose. She was utterly bewitched—not repulsed."

My heart squeezed, a gentle furrow in my brow. *No,* he couldn't possibly have been so cruel.

For the first time, Eoin's smile flickered with uncertainty, like a child caught wandering away from his parents. "It was my betrothal gift to her. A token of my devotion."

I ripped my hand from his and stood, trembling. "You gave it to her."

A flurry of images crossed my mind—all of them involving the many violent ways I could end him now.

No, not him.

Her. *Her.*

But he was here, and he had confessed to a deed of such monstrous disrespect that I couldn't rid myself of the inclination to hurt him. I had to get away from him—had to stop myself before I sent his soul to where I could never again reach.

"Róisín," Eoin said, rising to his feet. He raised his hands as though to soothe a frightened animal.

"Step away from me."

"Just help me understand—"

"You vile human!" I hissed. The words burned like bile in my mouth. I couldn't be sure if I even meant it. All I saw was red, and that rose, and my Eoin cradling some common maid in his arms, where *I* was meant to be.

When I took a quick step back, he surged forward to stop me from leaving. A hand seized my shoulder, wrenching me around.

"Róisín, *please*—wait!"

At once, a root burst from the earth, catching Eoin's ankle like a viper's strike. He fell hard, catching himself on his forearms, directly upon spindly brambles that had not been there moments before.

The tension shattered, silence spreading like a fog. No birdsong. No rustle of a breeze. There was only *me*.

Cursing in pain, Eoin pushed himself up carefully. Drops of his blood hit the ground. I quaked from the rush of energy that burst through my core. The earth drank his blood greedily—*I* drank it greedily through the roots beneath us, though he couldn't know it.

So much like the day he had cursed me with more consciousness and desire than I could bear.

The brambles receded into the ground. Eoin regarded me with wide eyes. I wanted to gash him deeper, let him bleed out until every last bit of him belonged to the forest, but—no. I couldn't. Especially not when he looked at me with such concern on his beautiful face.

I breathed shakily. My bare feet were silent on the mossy ground as I approached him. "I didn't mean—"

Eoin flinched when I reached for him. I stopped short, hating the pinch of emotion in my voice. "Let me see, please."

Kneeling, I extended a hand once more. Eoin met my gaze, relenting. I gently pulled his hands onto my lap, turning the palms up to expose the wounds along his arms. The gashes were many, but most were not deep—just painful enough to remind him of my power here.

I bowed down, pressing my lips to the first wound. Eoin's breath hitched, but he did not pull away. So I continued, kissing every cut in silence until his skin had mended under my intention, and only a few tears in his clothes remained.

"I'm sorry," Eoin breathed. "I upset you."

I shook my head. "Forgive me. I forgot myself. Feeling is... It doesn't come naturally to my kind, Eoin." I met his gaze. "And you make me feel a storm inside me when I'm near you."

His brow knit, but he gave a cautious nod, as though understanding—or trying to. He watched me with that look—the one torn between keeping me at arm's length and pouncing on me.

Then, I saw it—a line of crimson curling under the shadow of his jaw. Guilt tightened its vice. Another injury from my outburst.

"You're still bleeding," I murmured, brushing the reddened area. "May I?"

There was a pause before I received a gruff nod. I moved in slowly. Eoin shivered as I brushed tangled strands of his hair back from his throat. I said nothing more before pressing my lips to the gash. His skin was so *warm* there. The motion was reverent, penitent—but I dwelled too long. My mouth lingered there over the healed skin, my body anchored against his. I was suddenly aware of our bodies; how I had crawled halfway into his lap, and Eoin was rigid, but not with fear now. My very realization seemed to make something shift in the air, and the silence rippled with a tension that crackled in every inch between us.

Eoin turned his head, ever so slightly, and our mouths were so close, I could practically hear the question demanding to be answered.

"We can't." His voice was a gravelly, strained thing that made my stomach flutter.

But his calloused hands were on my waist—not pushing me away, but holding me in place. His breath deepened.

"But you want to," I whispered back.

Eoin's fingers twitched against me, trembling as he felt the curves hidden beneath my gossamer slip. I should not have felt such heat in my belly—I was not meant to experience such primal lust. My sisters and I were guardians of this sacred forest, not common whores.

But when his touch drifted beneath the hem of my gown, I thought I might perish from the raw pleasure of it.

And then he closed the space, pressing his lips to mine.

This kiss was not tentative or apologetic—it was fierce, bruising. It was *want*. There was a hunger blossoming, restraint severing. I felt him give in to me, piece by piece.

My hands moved to the strong column of his throat, plucking at the collar of his wool shirt, exposing more of his skin, flushed and warm. I trailed kisses down his neck, claiming him and tasting him with every touch. He crushed his arms around me like he might be able to fuse us together—moonlight and sunlight colliding.

A simple shift of weight, and then Eoin had rolled over me, my legs spread beneath his. Willing prey to his hunt. The strap of my gown slipped off my shoulder, and he pounced to kiss my exposed shoulder.

The forest crackled with life around us—saplings pushing from the frozen ground. Crimson roses blossomed, carpeting the ground in a widening radius with every moan that passed my lips.

"Say my name," I demanded, though it came out as little more than a whisper.

He did. He said it like a prayer to the stars. Again and again. A feral glint seared his gaze—I adored the animal in him. Something dark and wild that matched the monster in me. He was greedy in the way all humans would look at a creature like me—to keep me as his own personal secret like some sinful source of pride.

For him alone, I would gladly chain myself.

"Don't lie anymore," I panted. "Don't pretend you don't wish to possess me. To claim me as yours."

Eoin's hand hitched beneath the fabric pooling around my thighs, squeezing me hard enough to pull air from my lungs. I wound my hands into his hair, arching into him. We were both breathless and reckless in the same way, transforming between the trees around us. We were wicked and wonderful and—*stars*, I could scarcely think with his body pressed over mine.

"You belong to me," I said. "You always have. Just as I am yours. You see?"

His lips were still on mine when I felt him remember the world around us. A pause, a tremor of consideration. Slowly, he pulled away to look down at me like a man coming up for air before drowning. Locks of golden-brown hair fell over his face.

Come back. Come back to me.

"No, I-I belong to someone else," he said slowly.

I stared at him, my lips still swollen and waiting. The energy between us still hummed, but its rhythm was broken. Eoin's gaze darted around the clearing, remembering where he was and catching briefly on the field of roses my desire had conjured around us. The blossoms stirred in an icy breeze, carrying their sweet aroma around us.

"I gave her my word," he went on, his voice thick. "I promised her I'd come back to her."

Eoin pried himself off me, though not without some reluctance. The winter air cut against me where his body had been moments ago.

My chest ached like it was collapsing in on itself. I scrambled to sit up, not bothering to adjust my disheveled gown as I touched Eoin's leg.

"Your soul is starving for something that girl can never give you," I told him.

Eoin gazed at me for a long time—just long enough to give me hope. "You and I... We're not the same. How could we ever...?" He shook his head and swallowed hard, shame replacing lust. When his eyes met mine again, something had shuttered in him. Something closed off to me forever.

"I'm sorry," he whispered. "I won't make any excuses."

He laid his hand over mine. "Please reconsider allowing her into the forest. I want you to be a part of my life. But she's to be my bride soon."

Love was an abomination. How could something that made me want to sing and screech with laughter now turn to poison in my chest? I felt like I was dying as he slowly pulled himself to his feet and straightened his clothes, putting space between us.

A tear rolled off my chin. I caught it in my palm and closed my hand into a tight fist. I felt it harden within my grasp. As I unfurled my fingers, a perfect little gem sat in the middle of my palm, winking in the light. I stood, holding it out to Eoin.

"Please, stay with me," I said in a hushed voice.

Eoin accepted the gem, turning it in the winter sunlight between his finger and thumb. He regarded it with a dark scrutiny he no longer masked. Did he understand? Did he see the value of the gift I offered? The endless joy we could have if he would only say *yes*?

"Brianna is waiting for me," he said.

Giving me one last, shadowed look, Eoin turned. I let him walk away.

And in the space where he had almost chosen me, I sank to the ground and wept.

6

That wicked woman is not coming into my woods, I thought viciously as I stalked through the trees.

My siblings kept their distance, but the weight of their stares followed me through the rustling leaves. They sensed my pain through the pulsing roots of the forest. They pitied me. Perhaps they were hopeful that my undoing would revert me to my former, dispassionate ways, before Eoin.

But my temper only rose as I thought about his absence over the past weeks. He promised to return regularly again now that his courtship was complete, but that had to be a lie. He was giving his life to another. Soon, he wouldn't stop to even consider a stroll through the forest, burdened by a wife and mewling children and *their* children yet to come. A new life. One that would burn brightly at first and then extinguish.

I gave a wail so mournful that my sisters even attempted to soothe me. The forest, layered with hushed and sweet voices, fell over me in comfort, but I brushed them away and ran.

I didn't realize *where* I was running until the trees began to thin and I felt the familiar resistance of the forest's edge. Thatched roofs came into view between the trees across the meadow.

I stilled, letting the sounds of human life wash over me. The faint murmur of conversations. Everything felt painfully crisp, and I squeezed my eyes shut.

"This way, Aisling!" A warm, calloused hand in mine, pulling me. Brambles snaring on a gown. The smell of dahlias thick in the air.

Memories. *My* memories?

My throat felt tight at the violent wave of emotions. Joy and grief, fear and exhilaration.

As I watched the distant figures of humans milling about their duties, a heavy throb of lucidity stirred within me. I was steps away from the village paths and yet a world apart. For the first time in many years, the question drifted into focus: *What had happened to me?*

A contemplative wind gusted through the woods, caressing the locks of hair that hung over my shoulders like fingers combing through tenderly.

We're not meant to bear such things, my sisters said.

They were all around in the trees. Over a dozen of them—ivory skin that glowed in the sunlight and pale hair sapped of all color. They watched from trees above, or peering behind the trunks of gnarled oaks even older than us. Their whispering rose into an endless hum of energy.

Go no further, sister, they begged. Their urgency heightened as though they meant to protect me from something horrid, but none of them would dare to draw so close to the forest's edge, where I stood.

And then, my eyes fell upon what they attempted to shield me from. A glimmer on the ground made my throat run dry. The frantic whispering came to an abrupt stop. Wrapped in silence, I considered turning around, pretending I had never seen it.

Stepping forward, I plucked the cold, hard gem from the bed of winter decay.

My tear.

Hands trembling, I nearly let it slip from my fingers. Perhaps he dropped my gift by accident. He was mortal, after all—prone to clumsiness and carelessness.

Or he meant to discard it, one of my sisters dared to hiss. *A rejection of your gift. A quiet promise to never return.*

A rustle of agreement shivered through the forest, trying to draw me back to safety. To make me believe that Eoin wanted nothing more to do with me. To forget him. But rather than flee back into the embrace of my home, I latched onto the enraging idea that Eoin would hold hate for me within his heart.

I wanted to howl. I wanted to rip him apart.

All I could see was the guilt etched upon his face when he'd pushed me away. The desire was there. It *was*. I just needed to help him see it.

The rejection wasn't his own doing. It was the woman who took him away from me. A traveler, he said. A hateful wraith—perhaps even a creature sent by the Wild Hunt to torment me, to rip away the one villager unafraid of the forest and weaken us.

Stay, my sisters begged. *Should the woman be a wraith, leave the mortal to his fate.*

But my anguish was more powerful than their pleas could hope to be, drowning out their beckons. The ground around me erupted in bright green leaves that had no place in the dead of winter. Brambles crackled forth from the bushes, dripping with purple berries.

Pale faces watched with wide eyes. Their whispers grew louder until my voice drowned them all out.

"I will not stand idly by any longer," I proclaimed. "This wraith—this *witch*... Eoin needs me to watch over him."

But I could not traverse into the village in this form. I would be unprotected, slaughtered. Superstitions could so easily turn to violence—I had witnessed it countless times. I would need an illusion, the type of magic that had gone untouched for decades. Such power was only used for keeping the mortals in their place.

The thought of donning a mortal disguise filled me with revulsion, but I could not bear to retreat—not with this hatred that pulsed through me like the fierce current of a thawed river. I could still feel Eoin's breath against me—the promise of eternity. The forest could not contain me any longer.

It will hurt terribly, one of my sisters reminded me—her voice a whisper in the wind.

I couldn't bring myself to care. Physical pain might be a welcome reprieve from the cavernous ache of loneliness. And besides, who were they to judge me after the countless wicked things that had unfolded at their hands over the centuries?

I summoned the magic, shutting my eyes to focus. I willed the illusion of life—freckled, sun-kissed skin, color in my cheeks, a rich brunette to my hair.

When I opened my eyes again, my sisters were gone. Surely they could not bear the sight of me now. Perhaps they were right. The magic had left me breathless in a way my usual power did not, as though even my own body protested me.

I turned my hands over, marveling at my handiwork. The illusion was perfect, but a strange ache swirled in as I touched the simple chemise dress that had replaced my opalescent gown. There was something so familiar about the way it fell over me. A part of me wanted to chase that feeling to the end of the earth—to remember.

But the illusion would only last for hours. I had to be swift.

Gathering myself, I took my first step out of the forest. White-hot pain shot through my leg. I howled, keeling onto my side along the cobblestone path. I looked at my bare feet, feeling for the wound. But there was no blood—not even the faintest scratch.

I looked up at the towering oaks, feeling the winter's bite more harshly as I recalled my sisters' warning.

It will hurt.

Breathing heavily, I rose to my feet and took another step. The pain shot through my right foot this time, nearly blinding me. I groaned, nearly falling to my knees yet again. Every step felt like stepping on a blade.

Eoin would thank me someday, when he knew what lengths I had taken to protect him.

Choking back sobs, I set my gaze toward the cluster of snow-dusted roofs and set down the village path.

7

My body begged for mercy with each step forward. If I had ever felt such physical agony, the memory was deeply buried beneath the span of many mortal lifetimes.

Bit by bit, the land became tamer. I paid no mind to the domesticated animals and farmers at the outskirts of the village, forcing my eyes straight ahead for fear of looking back. But as the dirt path hardened into cobblestone beneath the snow, my disconnection from the forest deepened like a blade to the bone.

Trembling, I dared to peer over my shoulder. The tree line enticed me, barren branches spread like open arms. The promise of relief, however, appeared more like a prison. Like a waiting tomb.

Tomb.

I wavered, my legs pulsing with a new ache, like I had been running for ages.

Skirts tangling my legs, threatening to trip me. The cold air stinging upon each breath, like icicles scraping my throat and lungs. Branches and twigs scraping my skin like claws,

opening cuts. Blood dripping, creating a trail, leading him straight to me—

Clutching my head, I blinked hard. The faster I chased the memories, the further they ran, until I could scarcely remember what I'd been picturing at all. Like a fading dream, though I had never dreamt in this lifetime.

I forced myself forward.

The village had progressed much further than I had assumed. The heart of it had been hidden from my perch at the tree line all these years. Even in winter, the market was teeming with mortals—far more than I had glimpsed from the forest's edge.

Too many, I thought disdainfully.

In the busy square, some curious eyes lingered upon me, but Eoin's claim of travelers must have been grander than he let on. These villagers didn't appear shaken by an unfamiliar face, and none stopped to question my presence.

That's right, look away. The continuous pain throbbing through my body was too great for me to pay much attention to an overly curious mortal.

As I began to devote attention to the thought of tracking Eoin, worry trickled through me. How long could I remain this far from the forest before I perished? Would I feel when my power was sapped to a flicker? Or would I simply blink and become nothingness? For all I knew, I had already seen Eoin's face for the final time.

The thought made staying upright impossible. I staggered into one of the market stalls to catch myself.

"Away with you!" the man behind the counter snapped. Fabrics were strewn about his stall. Even as I struggled to straighten myself, he glared like I was no more than a troublesome pest. "Die elsewhere, girl—*away*."

I scowled weakly. "Pray you never find yourself within reach of the forest," I said in a guttural voice I scarcely recognized.

"Why is that?"

If he knew my power, he would cower in fear. I pictured myself driving him to madness, making him pluck out his own eyes to feed them to a wolf. But here, such a threat would mark me as nothing more than a madwoman.

My vision went spotty as I pushed myself away from the stall. I was ready to sink to the ground when arms wrapped around me from behind. Snarling, I struggled, but the arms were strong and brought me to my feet.

"Are you alright?" a voice asked in my ear.

I froze.

Eoin.

Once I was steady, he circled to face me worriedly. The sight of his face made my breath catch.

"Miss?" he asked, slower. "Are you alright?"

His frown of concern was so genuine that I nearly sank back into his arms. But though his gaze was warm, it held no familiarity. This was the kindness of a stranger.

"I'm—" I started to say, but my breaths became too labored to speak.

Eoin grasped my upper arms, his worry deepening. "You're freezing. Wait here—please."

I observed in quiet amazement as he bought a cloak from the disgruntled man at the stall. Eoin tossed the fabric around my shoulders and tied it in front. I snatched his hands before he could pull away. Although the cloak did little to ease my suffering, my shivering lessened.

"Thank you," I whispered.

"I wish I could afford something thicker for you," he said, gently pulling his hands away. "Are you well, Miss? What is your name?"

"Aisling," I breathed, the name spilling out naturally.

"Where did you come from? Are you with those traders from Donegal?"

I shook my head. His brow furrowed, eyes darting around us thoughtfully. "So you must live nearby. Do you have someone who can help you, lass? You don't look well."

"I'm alone," I said, swallowing hard. "And I don't need healers or a *liaig*. I'm here to help *you*."

He gave me a strange look, scanning me up and down—the frail stranger who had staggered into his village without even a cloak on her back. "I'll confess I don't know what you mean. You... We've never even met."

Spots danced in my vision as I took two excruciating steps closer to him. "Let me show you," I rasped.

His eyes widened slightly, and for a moment, I wondered if he recognized me beyond the illusion. He had to, even in a small way. After years of visiting me in the forest, Eoin *knew* me, the way I knew everything about him.

"Eoin, there you are, lad!" Someone broke away from the bustling vendors and craftsmen boasting their wares in the square to cut toward us. He was a hefty man with a scraggly blond beard and simple clothes, belted at the waist. He clapped Eoin on the back, giving him a well-meaning shake.

"Come along, the tavern's packed to the gills. They'll be waiting on you for the toast by now." His grin dropped as he looked at me. "Who's this wee thing?"

"That remains to be seen," Eoin said, though not unkindly. He smiled and gave the man an amicable shove toward the tavern that sat on the corner, with ribbons hanging from the wooden rafters. "Tell them I'm just steps away. I know better than to keep Collin from his ale."

They shared a chuckle at this, and with another curious glance at me, the man departed. Impatience resided in Eoin's gaze when he focused back on me, but he seemed to push it down in favor of hospitality.

"It appears I'm late to my own betrothal party." He backed toward the tavern, rubbing the back of his neck. "It's nothing extravagant, but there will be food and warmth, a bit of ale. Perhaps I'll see you there, if you like." He smiled over his shoulder and gave me a small wave before striding off purposefully.

Always so kind, my Eoin. I would not lose him. I willed my legs to move, following after what was mine by right.

As I trailed after him, my racing heart distracted me from the white-hot pain that shot up my legs. Today was his engagement party—and even on such a momentous occasion, mere hours beforehand, he had come to see *me* in the forest.

The thought of what we had nearly done there made my mouth turn dry.

Why else would he do such a thing if he didn't truly care for me? If he didn't *want* me to do something so drastic to follow after him? He was a lost soul—and this wretched woman was leading him astray, away from what he desired. Even under her illusion, a part of him must have wanted me to see this madness and put a stop to it.

Eoin hid his discomfort expertly as he entered the tavern, dimples flashing as he smiled widely at the crowd at the threshold. I watched him be pulled inside, into the roar of a welcoming throng. His concern for the feeble stranger he'd encountered evaporated from his face.

Breathing heavily, I leaned my weight against the wide window at the front of the building. The door was inches away, but I could not bring myself to set a foot inside despite Eoin's invitation. There was relief in finally holding still for a moment; the pain eased, if only a little bit.

I watched the celebration unfold. Despite the crudeness of it, unmistakable joy flowered in the air. Mince pies, barley loaves, and poached pears were laid on a wide table. Amber bottles were lined up in a row, plucked up to ensure every goblet was brimming.

My stomach twisted, my fingers pressed to the weathered exterior of the building—was this *grief?*

There was longing and loneliness, yes—but something more, too.

Have I been here before?

Aisling.

Where had that name come from? It was too simple, too *mortal*, to have any right to feel so familiar to me. I must have heard it on the lips of a human who had wandered near the forest, or perhaps from Eoin when he spoke of his village.

The thought of him sent me searching for his face through the packed tavern. My eyes landed upon him, seated at the head of the center table. His hand rested upon the wooden surface, fingers entwined with those of a woman's. His smiling gaze was fixed on the man who'd intercepted him in the market. Glasses were raised as the man gave a speech.

I paid his words little mind as my gaze slid to Eoin's bride—*Brianna*. My lips curled back. She was squeezing Eoin's hand, practically pinning it to the table. Her long brunette hair was plaited with ribbons and flowers—*flowers* torn from the earth to feed her vanity. Her cornflower-blue dress stood out brightly amongst the other fabrics surrounding her.

The tavern erupted with cheers and applause as the speech came to an end. Several men clapped Eoin on the back after they all drank deeply from their goblets.

Amidst the uproarious noise, I forced myself to slip through the door. The cacophony, so grating and utterly human, nearly made me retreat. But I couldn't leave Eoin. I pulled the hood of my gifted cloak up, dropping into the empty end of a bench where I could go unnoticed.

As I sank with relief, a weight in my simple gown's pocket caught my attention. Reaching in, I felt the skin of smooth, plump berries. I could picture them in my mind's eye—bright purple, perfectly ripe. I could scarcely recall plucking them from the bush.

Sudden quiet fell over the tavern, startling me more than the raucous noise.

An elderly woman's voice broke the silence. "Take each other's hand and hold steady—very good."

Every eye was fixed on Eoin and his bride-to-be, who stood at the front of the tavern. The elderly woman—I had never seen a human so advanced in age—began wrapping a braided cord around their hands. It knotted around their knuckles, their wrists, their forearms nearly to the elbow.

"May you forever be one," the woman said, her frail voice carrying to every corner of the tavern. "In love, in loyalty, for all time to come."

My throat tightened around the threat of a shriek.

A handfasting ceremony.

The image and its name wavered on the edge of a far-away memory, much like everything else that had felt familiar since leaving the forest. The weight of the ceremony sat upon my heart like a jagged stone. I wanted to push past the villagers and rip the cord away, shred it into pieces to free Eoin from being bound to this woman.

A small noise did escape me, but another round of cheers masked it as the cord was fully fastened.

Brianna leaned up to kiss him eagerly, and I begged Eoin to pull away, to realize that this was all wrong. But his lips met hers, and he pulled her closer like he was starving for her taste.

How can he bear to kiss such a disgusting creature, I thought. *She's tricked him. He doesn't want this—any of this.*

The gentle pluck of music was replaced with a riotous duo of fiddles. Dancing spread through the room like it was contagious, and Eoin led them all. His lean, toned frame cut a striking figure even in a crowd. Brianna clutched at him, shrieking with laughter as they stepped in time. His movements were untethered, light-footed as a stag. I couldn't help but compare the way he'd danced with me those months ago in the pond—slow and restrained, like he was walking in a dream.

As more of the villagers circled into the dance, I stood, snatching up a forgotten goblet on the table beside me. I clutched the polished wood tighter with every stab of pain that came from my careful footsteps. It was getting worse. How much time did I have left?

I stole a glance out the window, where the slope of the forest lay in wait beyond the thatched rooftops. My heart skipped a beat when I saw pinpricks of light in the branches. A perfect, unnatural line along the oaks.

My sisters, watching and waiting for me.

Stomach twisting, I stared back stoically. They could not be pleased by this. But they would never understand. Eoin was unlike the other mortals here—and needed me to keep him from harm.

Still, they watched.

I nearly barreled right into another dancing couple as I uneasily tore my gaze away from the window. I dodged around a barrel of flour, keeping to the walls.

Pieces of conversation caught my ear, and I allowed myself to watch from my new position out of the way. Eoin and his bride-to-be spoke with their guests between dances about how her dowry would be of great help through the winter months and beyond. Their gratitude for the wedding gifts was already set upon their doorstep.

The winter—that must be why he chose to wed now. He was marrying this girl out of desperation, out of the sheer need to survive the winter thanks to the provisions the wedding would bring. Shadows curled in my chest at the thought of what I could have provided—how much more I *should* have offered Eoin before this wraith swept in and convinced him she was worthy of his affection.

A guest with ale-reddened cheeks and plaited red hair embraced them both, asking if they hoped for a son or daughter. A snarl built in my throat as Brianna smiled widely and exchanged a look with Eoin.

"My family has been blessed with many sets of twins," she answered in that grating, lyrical voice. "Perhaps we will have both."

The rest of the room didn't understand, but that smile on Eoin's face was strained, full of regret and fear at the thought of such a commitment.

Another stab of pain shot through me—this time, a cold sweat broke out on my brow. It was like the edge of a blade had been dragged up the backs of my legs, burying the hilt in my lower back. I gasped hard enough to turn heads.

Another glance at the window. The sun had lowered, and my sisters were no longer on the treeline. Somehow, that only felt worse. I looked down at my hands, where the illusion of life still thrummed weakly.

I'm running out of time.

Suddenly, the air felt too thick and stale with the smell of too many things at once—sweat and ale, herbed bread and smoky embers. *Air.* I needed fresh air. In the sea of faces, I could no longer spot Eoin's golden-brown hair.

I found a side door and made a quick exit, gasping in the clean, biting air outside. There was a small courtyard behind the tavern, bearing a cobblestone well, several barrels of food and mead, and a wall of firewood stacked by the door. And ahead—

Home.

The border of this part of the village touched the very edge of a meadow that led into massive trees. Their ancient trunks loomed just metres away, with inky blackness between each like strips of midnight. It was a darkness that wanted to eat—and I knew with every fiber of my being I needed to be consumed by it, for it was *me.*

Time to return, the snow-laced wind whispered, brushing back the hood of my cloak, pulling me forward.

"I'm *trying,*" I huffed under my breath.

I would come back for Eoin. I would save him and remind him of what he truly desired.

Wine sloshed from my goblet as I staggered toward the trees. My knees gave out, forcing me to slam against the cobblestone well in the center of the courtyard.

"You should know better than to hide, Aisling."

Footsteps on autumn leaves. Dirt under my fingernails. Gasping for air—

I pulled myself up, making it past the fence that separated the tavern from the dirt path at the back.

"Please don't do this."

Something hard and heavy on my throat. "You haven't left me a choice."

The memory was a wildfire ripping through the careful walls of my sanity. I cried out, waves of terror and rage that didn't belong to me crashing through my chest.

I was the forest, and the forest was me.

But I'd never had a choice.

"Please don't do this." My own voice echoed in my mind.

I was nothing more than a *prisoner*. A monster chained in the very place I had—

The door to the tavern opened, and someone stepped out. Cornflower blue caught the corner of my eye before I turned and saw Brianna, a bucket under her arm. She hooked it onto the pulley at the wall, her freckled cheeks still flushed, and a little melody hummed under her breath.

When she caught me staring, her smile became a shriek.

"Oh, *Brigid above,* you frightened me," she exclaimed, clasping a hand to her mouth. I supposed I must have been a sight—pale, trembling, with my hair bedraggled. After a moment to compose herself, Brianna masked her fright with a smile. "Have you come in for a bite of food yet? We've plenty to go around, and then some."

"Yes," I said.

The single rasped word sat between us like a canyon, with only the faint murmur of the celebration carrying on behind the tavern walls breaking our silence. I could see the dancing had become more vigorous since I left, as whiskey began to flow alongside the ale.

Brianna frowned faintly, something maternal and deeply misplaced crossing her features. I didn't need her charity. She was like a child approaching a god.

She crossed around the well to reach me, scanning me up and down.

"You look quite pale," she said. "You must be freezing. Won't you join us inside again, friend?"

She extended a hand to touch my arm, and I fought the urge to bite it off finger by finger down to the bone.

You took him from me, I wanted to hiss at her. *If not for you, I wouldn't be alone.*

But I forced a more pleasant, apologetic tone and leaned away from her. "I must be off. I...I am unwell." Breathing heavily, I peeked at the goblet still clutched in my hand. I raised it to her and softened my gaze. "But I cannot forgo the opportunity to offer a toast to such a kind bride. Please—have the rest. To your good health."

She pressed a hand to her breast and shook her head. "Nonsense. Enjoy your drink and rest well, my friend."

Her refusal sent anger prickling up my spine. Perhaps she suspected something—but no, that dull face was emptier than a tree hollow. This creature before me was no wraith. She was a simple, mortal girl who had stolen the life that should have been mine—unworthy for the likes of Eoin.

I pressed the goblet into her hands, kissing her knuckles with all the tenderness of a lover. "Please," I said softly, "it is my gift."

I could scarcely recall the journey back to my home. My next moment of awareness came when I set foot in the boundaries of the forest, and my surroundings consumed me like the loving embrace of a relieved mother.

The illusion faded, and though the pain ebbed, the exhaustion of the experience did not. I sank onto the earth and curled onto my side, trembling. The frozen earth was cool and comforting against my cheek.

My sisters gathered around me, equally cool voices and hands welcoming my return to where I belonged. As I lay there, I couldn't shake the familiarity. And though it was still blurry and distant, a memory struck me with a heated blow.

Why did I feel like I had been here in this exact position before?

A whimper rose at the back of my throat, and when I peeked my eyes open, I expected to find the forest floor around me soaked in red.

But there was nothing.

And I was safe.

8

Light frost still covered the barren branches of my favorite perch weeks later. This winter was harsher than most, but I did not feel the cold. It wasn't the elements that would harm me—it was the all-too-human longing searing a constant hole in my chest that I was certain would do me in.

Time passed, and I forced myself to reckon with the reality that this loneliness was here to stay. Day by day, I drifted from clearing to clearing with my sisters, forcing myself to remember the eon I had already spent here observing, perfecting, and protecting alongside them before Eoin had entered the forest. Before his blood had touched the same soil as mine.

He would become a beautiful, painful memory. Centuries would pass before the image of his face was entirely erased from my mind.

No, I thought. *Even then, I will remember him. It will take thousands of years, and still I will know him.*

I was plaiting my sister's hair with snowdrop blossoms when I felt a disturbance in the air. The wind shivered. Goldfinches burst into flight, scattering into the gray sky.

Someone had entered the woods.

I stood, letting my touch drift from her hair. My sister seized my wrist, her ice blue eyes wide and cutting—

Do not go.

I wrenched away, pushing onward as though in a trance.

I must.

Before I knew it, my legs had taken me to my clearing—crawling along gnarled branches, leaping from tree to tree, bare feet padding along frozen earth—where my favorite oak tree unfurled toward the ground, its ancient branches like an outstretched hand clawing for freedom it would never find.

The glow of a lantern resting upon the ground caught my eye first.

A human knelt at the edge of the creek—*my human.*

My idiotic heart leapt at the hope that I would not have to suffer centuries alone to forget him. Eoin had come back for me, at last.

A soft sound cut through the meadow, and it took me a moment to realize he was crying.

I slowed my steps, not making myself visible yet as I circled to get a better look at him. Eoin had never once dared to visit me in the night. He was slumped with one shoulder against our tree, his eyes bruised with lack of sleep and swollen from crying. A haze of stubble darkened his jaw as though he hadn't shaved in days. His stare was fixed on nothing in particular, still shuddering out half-formed sobs that shook his shoulders.

Oh, how he suffered without me.

I approached from behind, touching his head delicately as I lifted the magic that cloaked me. Eoin started, looking back at me in the lantern's light. My heart gave another odd lurch at that empty stare—a hollowness that didn't look like *him*.

"My Eoin," I all but whispered when I found my voice. "What pains you so?"

He attempted to form the words several times. I carefully allowed my expression to crumple when he finally choked out, "She's dead."

Somehow, uttering those words seemed to ground him back into reality. "She was taken in the night with no warning. One moment, she was laughing by the fire in my arms. The next..." His expression became faraway again as he was tossed back into that memory. "We brought her to the *liaig,* but none of his herbs or tonics could turn the sickness. Brianna wept of a fire in her chest, but it was a fever the healer had not seen before. No one had. Three nights we stayed by her side, and still she—she slipped away."

Eoin's last words choked off. As he broke down, I wrapped my arms around him and murmured words of comfort. While he wept into my gown, I was glad that he could not see the soft curve of my smile. He allowed me to stroke his hair just like I had done countless times before. At last, our world was settling back into what it should have been all along.

I forced tears to spill down my cheeks. Carefully catching one in my palm, I felt it harden against my skin.

"Eoin," I whispered. His sniffling went silent when I offered my open hand—a tiny opalescent gemstone awaited in the pit of my palm. "It's time. You need not be alone. Don't suffer this anguish any longer."

I awaited the satisfaction of watching relief flood his face—that I would graciously allow him back into my life after he betrayed me so cruelly. But the hesitancy in his expression quickly gave way to a flicker of fear—and then, a hardness that rivaled a wildfire.

Face contorting, he struck upward, seizing me by the throat. The gemstone flew from my hand as he launched to his feet and loomed against me, pressing me against the tree. A small, curved blade was at my throat, ripped from his belt. The sting of cold metal sent a jolt of shock racing through my entire body.

"It was *you*," he said in a guttural voice. "I know it was—don't you dare lie to me."

His eyes were bloodshot, still flayed with fresh tears. I wanted to trace the path of each drop that streaked across his sun-kissed skin with my tongue.

"Let me go," I gasped. *You're breaking my heart.*

Eoin bared his teeth, pressing the dagger closer. The blade did not hold pure iron—just enough to convince him it would make a difference.

"Some thought it was a wind-illness," he gritted out. "Others say she angered the gods. I don't know how—*how* it was that you did it, but...I know it was you. I should have been wed today, but instead I walked my love to her tomb."

"Grief has clouded your senses," I said with what little breath I could draw.

I struggled for leeway to buck him off me, but Eoin's taller frame easily corralled me back into place against the unforgiving bark. I could feel the hard-earned strength from his years laboring as a craftsman, the way he could easily throw me about if I allowed him. There was a new gleam surfacing in his eyes, as though he was just realizing this, too.

Unbidden memories of running, sobbing, *hiding* cut across my mind—the girl I had once been. I clenched my jaw and silenced the mourning that threatened to unravel me.

"No—I've never been more clear of mind." Eoin sneered as though seeing something hideous instead of my perfected, ethereal beauty. "The Wild Hunt is fast approaching."

My eyes widened, and I stopped struggling. His words sank in slowly, painfully.

"You...you brought hunters here?"

The blaze of satisfaction in his eyes was answer enough. "They're close now. I saw them coming. They know precisely what to do with the likes of you. A *monster*." He leaned forward, the last words brushing against my cheek.

Enough.

Something severed in me, something hungry and animal and terrified to die a second time. I could no longer afford to be gentle.

I slammed both my palms against the tree at my back. The oak's roots burst from the ground, writhing at unnatural angles like starving serpents. Despite the winter, the clearing erupted with feverish green. Vines, coarse and covered in thorns, sprouted from the many chasms now littering the soil, twisting around Eoin's ankles.

Blood, the forest roared to him. *There will be blood.*

He shouted, jumping away from me. He slashed at the vines with that pathetic little blade of his, and I winced as he successfully severed a pair of vines. I narrowed my eyes, honing my target. The roots slithered fast, faster than Eoin could react. They knocked him to the ground, winding over his arms and legs as he gasped for air. The dagger was lost, devoured by the mess of vines along the ground, along with the light from the lantern.

When Eoin was barely able to struggle against the earthen bindings, I approached him slowly, cloaked in shadows. Tree limbs parted, allowing only enough moonlight for him to see me—a beautiful, bloodthirsty creature of the forest with jagged branches haloing me overhead. Tears coursed freely down my cheeks, thudding gently onto the forest floor as gemstones.

"I am not a monster," I said, my voice returning to its quiet strength. "You see, I understand what I am now."

The vines parted for my every step to offer a cushion of the moss that lay beneath. I knelt over him, smiling gently even though a terrified sweat glistened on his brow and turned his gaze wild. A single lock of his hair was strewn across his forehead. I tucked it back into place, unflinching when he growled in his throat, trying to lean away from me.

"My life was taken here, on the very ground you lie upon," I explained. "The forest took me in, gave me a new life. A lonely life—one without passion and *true* purpose... Until you found me. Until you bled upon the ground where I died. You made me remember what it was like to *feel*."

I smiled widely at him, breathless. Finally, I could tell him everything. Even speaking of it, I felt every emotion with keen, intoxicating fervor.

"You made me know desire again. Joy, lust, and heartache. You had no idea the gift and curse you set upon me." My gaze briefly lost focus as I considered the soil beneath our bodies—and who lay beneath it. "But other things came with it. Memories. Terrible fragments of another life. What it felt like to perish, to claw for survival while my soul is ripped away."

"Róisín," Eoin rasped in a thready semblance of a command. "Release me. *Now.*"

I cupped his face between my hands, even as he gritted his teeth and tried to pull away. I held him steady, forcing his eyes to me.

"Don't you see? We are two souls entwined by the thread of destiny. The forest delivered you to me as a gift after all these years. A chance for me to love again—for *both* of us."

Eoin spat, catching me full on the cheek. I brushed it away, my gaze shuttering.

"I don't love you," Eoin growled. "I will die before ever loving a creature like you."

"And you dare to speak to me about lying?" My laugh was cold and hollow. I wove my fingers into his golden brown locks and gripped tightly, ignoring the hiss of pain as I drove his gaze back up. I hated that he forced my hand, but he was so *stubborn.* "Who forced you to return to this place day after day after I revealed myself to you? For *years*? No one but your own greed and infatuation."

Eoin breathed heavily, his silence prolonged this time. The fire in his gaze wavered as he gazed up at me. A part of him acknowledged the darkness in him that he had tried to deny day after day, as all humans did.

"Why me?" he finally asked. "I'm no one. Fix your obsession on someone else."

More tears welled up in my eyes—tears of *love* despite everything he had done to me. "Love does not offer a choice. It is devastating, all-consuming. You belong to me. And we can still be happy together. I can forgive everything."

"I don't want it. *Any* of it!" But his attempt at a heavy, commanding tone was no more than that—an attempt. He shut his eyes as though depriving me of his gaze might suffocate me from existence and make it easier to resist his feelings.

"Eoin." My voice caressed him with more tenderness than a mortal woman's touch could hope to achieve. "Don't be ashamed. We share the same want. You've done nothing wrong."

My fingertips brushed his lips, tracing down his jawline to rest upon the fluttering pulse of his neck. I pressed my forehead to his and did not move. My patience was rewarded when, slowly, he opened his eyes and lifted his gaze to meet mine.

"I can't," he whispered. "I can't."

His eyes flickered down as though finally registering how deep the neckline of my gown was, how kissable my lips were.

"Don't deny yourself," I breathed back. "You've waited so long."

Something gentle shivered beneath his stare—painfully familiar. *Temptation.*

As I lowered my lips to his, he did not pull away, did not protest. I breathed into him with terrible, wordless elation and sensed the instant that the tension fled his body. He kissed back—a tentative brush of lips that became a hungry, wanting thing. The brokenness of a man who had nothing left to lose.

The forest released him gradually—shoulders and arms first. His hands flew up to my neck at once, and for the briefest moment, I thought he was trying to strangle me again. But his touch moved higher, slipping into my silvery hair. Our mouths crushed together as his fingers wound their way through my tresses.

"There you are," I whispered as he paused for breath.

When the forest released the rest of his body, I leaned back to regard him. Bits of twigs and leaves clung to his hair and clothes like the forest couldn't bear to relinquish him entirely—the way I could scarcely bear it. As I drank him in, the calm in his expression morphed into something wicked and wanting.

"*Róisín,*" he groaned, surging forward to envelope me in his arms and find my lips once more. I returned his brutal affection with fervor.

He pushed my gossamer gown up, his hands desperately finding their way up my legs, squeezing my waist, and sliding back down again.

I unfastened his cloak, and he was seemingly unaffected by the chill of the night as he removed layer after layer. There was no cold. Nothing existed beyond us and the forest as he lay upon a bed of winter decay and shadows, and invited me atop him with feverish desire.

I crawled slowly onto him, leaving a trail of kisses from his abdomen to his chest.

As I spread my knees and welcomed him into me, Eoin gave a choked noise of pleasure and threw his head back, fingers digging painfully into my hips. I savored the ache. Finally, he had accepted that I had rooted into the dark and hollow spaces of his soul—that we shared the same sinful pull.

Each passing second was a gift. Time had never sat still for me, but here and now, I committed every breath, every heartbeat to memory as we joined beneath the eyes of the forest.

The trees bent around us, oscillating in gentle sync with my storm of labored breathing. Branches groaned, echoing the pleasured sounds that escaped our lips.

"More," I moaned, my hips moving feverishly. "*More, Eoin.*"

More, more, more, the forest echoed in a sharp, cutting breeze. It was as hungry as I was.

Eoin's tunic had been shed, leaving his bare torso gleaming from exertion. One strong arm wrapped around me, flipping me beneath him. His thrusts became more punishing, filling me deeper.

"Nothing has ever felt like this," he panted. "No one."

His kiss was hard and claiming, like a starving man. I smiled against his full lips, moaning into his mouth before claiming his lower lip with my teeth. I bit down hard enough to make Eoin gasp. The coppery tang of blood blossomed on my tongue. Even still, this fervor only brought a wild glint in Eoin's eyes, like this was a challenge—and I wondered if my forwardness surprised him, even now.

He ducked, his lips against my neck—then teeth, delicately pinching my ivory skin. Taking everything from me that he had wanted to for so long.

He spilled over the edge with a vicious moan, a sound that made me shiver with pleasure. He rolled onto the ground where the forest had created a carpet of waxy green grass beneath us, seeming to notice this for the first time. I lay tucked against his bare chest, feeling our hearts hammer out the same feverish rhythm.

We were still lying there, trembling with the sin and the rightness of it, when I heard a faint call on the horizon. Voices. Many of them.

"The Wild Hunt," I breathed.

Eoin sat up beside me, losing a shaky breath. His wide eyes scanned the treeline that led down the rolling slope toward the village.

"What have I done?" he whispered.

I looked at his face in the moonlight, unable to tell if our sacred act was the abomination, or calling hunters to my home to spill my blood.

The possibility of the former couldn't sting me now.

In a minute more, neither would matter.

Not bothering to fix the straps of my gown, I stood up. The freshly blossomed grass was waxy and cool beneath my bare feet.

"Come." I extended a hand to Eoin, hauling him up.

As the glaze of lust in his eyes began to sober with fear, I squeezed his hand, pressing myself against his front.

"The only way out is forward," I said, my voice calm and quiet, as though the pricks of torchlight appearing between the trees were worlds away. A tear snaked down my cheek. I caught the droplet in my free hand, curling my fist around it. I pressed the sparkling gemstone into Eoin's calloused palm and closed his fingers around it.

"What more have you to lose?" I kissed his knuckles, peering up at him with a smile that offered everything.

There was something broken and vulnerable that latched onto my offer—rewarding my long, suffering patience. Eoin did not shy away from my unblinking gaze. He gazed down at the tear, eyes flickering toward the approaching hunters.

He knew as well as I what they would do to someone who had shared such an act with a creature like me.

He closed his hand around the gem firmly, his rough palm locked against mine with the other. I squeezed his hand, rising on my tiptoes to brush my lips against his.

"You won't leave me?" His question was a soft breath against my skin.

"Never," I whispered.

His steps followed in stride with mine, scarcely audible on the forest floor, allowing me to lead him deeper into the forest, where we could at last make an everlasting home together—walking right past the brambles stripped of their deep purple berries, only a few left dangling.

My heart swelled as the trees latticed above us, slowly blotting out the silvery moon overhead. I had always known Eoin was different. He would be far better than the other men before him, wouldn't be afraid the way they'd been when my gift made him new and incorruptible.

It wouldn't be long now.

And *finally*, he would be home with me.

EPILOGUE
THE WILD HUNT

Torchlight flickered in the biting chill of the winter air. Desmond's arm strained as he held his torch aloft, desperate to shed illumination on the snow-dusted branches. As a youth, Desmond had spent many summers in the Limerick woods, taking turns hiding between the trees and mocking battles with wooden swords, pretending himself a mighty warrior. He'd always considered himself at home in these sacred places where nature outnumbered man.

But these woods loomed around their riding party with a quiet that seemed too encompassing.

"You hear that?" he asked, glancing at the riders on his left.

The others had hunted under Druid Chereth for many years more than he, their faces flinty and marred by scars. Desmond already bore a weak left shoulder from the banshee they'd eliminated from Donegal Castle grounds last month. He knew his days were numbered toward a warrior's death—all of them were.

"I hear nothing," one replied gruffly.

Desmond nodded, his brow furrowing as he shifted in his saddle. "Exactly. It's *wrong*, somehow. Like the forest is—"

He bit off the words as though he might summon his very suspicion.

Like the forest is watching us back.

There were no birds. No movement in the undergrowth. Nothing. Only the lonely howl of the winter wind. The longer Desmond listened, the more he swore he heard whispering with every gust between crooked branches.

He stole a look at their leader, who rode at the back of the group. Druid Chereth was enveloped in a heavy black cloak with a draped hood that concealed the scarring across his right cheek. Even he looked on guard, slowing his black mare to a cautious amble.

The chill in the air burrowed deeper than winter. There was something ancient here, something that made it very clear they were unwanted.

A crack sounded—small and sharp, just ahead. Desmond barely had time to clutch at the reins before his horse let loose a fearful whinny and reared violently. He was thrown, hitting the frozen earth with a thud that knocked the wind out of him. His torch rolled from his hand, extinguished with a hiss as it landed on the frosted leaves.

Two other riders dismounted to help him, one calming the startled horse and leading it back into line with the others.

"You alright, lad?"

"I'm fine," Desmond grunted, pushing himself onto his side. He swept his tawny hair back out of his eyes, scanning the ground.

Something small glittered in the underbrush, nearly invisible in the flickering shadows cast by the dozen torches. On hands and knees, he crawled closer, straightening his fur-lined cloak so as not to impede his movements. It was a diamond—or a striking gem, at least. No bigger than the size of a grain of barley, hewn in a delicate, tapered shape.

Another glint in the dirt—yet another gem, nearly tucked under the roots of an oak tree. Desmond frowned at the peculiarity, looking for more. Was it a trail, leading somewhere?

He reached for the beckon of those iridescent facets. When he let his gaze rest heavily enough on them, he swore he could hear music, like a distant chime.

"Don't touch it!"

The growled command made Desmond reel back. Druid Chereth dismounted his horse in a movement strikingly swift for someone of his age. His hood billowed and fell as he strode toward the younger hunter, weaving between the hunting party.

He knelt, shoving Desmond back so he could get a closer look. He cursed loudly, bristling a response from many to raise their spears.

"What is it?" Desmond asked.

Chereth combed a hand through his ragged silver beard. "It's a token of death from a spirit. Rare, but not to be overlooked." He fixed Desmond with such a grave look that he felt his dinner turn in his stomach. "If you accept it, they'll come for you. The forest will claim you for itself."

"That thing can kill you?" Desmond asked, incredulous. It was such a delicate little trinket.

Chereth's eyes darkened. "Worse than death, lad. The soul will be chained for eternity—a precipice between life and death, where even Brigid above can't help you."

Desmond's face paled, but he gave a grim nod of understanding. And even still, a part of him *wanted* that stone.

"Iron for such spirits?" he asked.

Druid Chereth grunted, nodding as he unsheathed the iron sword at his hip. It was a custom piece, slightly curved and engraved with protective runes along its blade.

"Over here!" Another shout came a few meters away. Desmond followed the hunters who'd dismounted, finding a clearing that seemed ravaged by the gods themselves. It looked as though some beast had tunneled out from beneath the earth, with tree roots exposed and suspended like dying snakes. Between the jagged roots, a carpet of green grass peppered with flowers sprawled across the earth—an impossible oasis of snowdrops and roses amid the barren landscape. Desmond loosed an awed breath—he couldn't help it. It was as beautiful as it was terrifying. Most of the cursed creatures he'd encountered thus far were purely the latter.

One of the hunters was crouched at the base of the tree, prodding the end of his spear into the loosened soil. Desmond became aware of the odd, yellowed color of the objects protruding.

"There are remains here," the hunter announced. "Looks to be four bodies—maybe more. I can't tell how deep it goes."

"The craftsman?" Chereth asked.

Desmond's mind raced to connect to the letter they had received two days ago, scrawled in hurried strokes across the parchment. There was a grim sort of way Chereth said it, as though he had suspected along the journey they might not be quick enough to prevent his entanglement with the beast.

"You think the monster got to him?" Desmond asked, hoping he wasn't pushing his luck. Oftentimes, new-bloods weren't supposed to speak to Druid Chereth unless spoken to.

Chereth gave him an odd look, the corners of his mouth upturned in a grim smile. "Did you not find it curious that the man was able to provide such detail in his haste? Right down to the very glade we were to investigate."

He gestured around them, at the carnage tattering the forest ground.

Desmond's blood chilled. "He was entangled with the beast," he said quietly.

"You'd be surprised how often these things occur. If this is the creature I think it to be, even more so. They're sirens of the forest. Beautiful as they are devastating."

Desmond looked toward the others, still sifting through the remains. He couldn't stop thinking of the urgency of the note, demanding their aid at any cost.

"Is it—"

"No, I doubt it's our man. These are decades old," the other hunter said, analyzing the jawless skull in his hand. "But we will keep a wary eye."

Desmond plunged into the clearing, his boots sinking in against the strange grass. His stomach had grown stronger in his time hunting, but... *Sweet Brigid,* this was a nightmare incarnate. He brushed his hand over the ancient oak, gazing upward. A faint hum of energy pulsed through the air. *I am alive,* it seemed to say. *I feel you. I know you.*

He paused, feeling something damp on his palm. *Warm.*

Desmond held his hand toward the nearest torch. Others leaned in, murmuring as they caught sight of the crimson smeared across his hand.

"It's fresh," Desmond croaked, fumbling for his blade. "We can't have missed them by much."

He locked eyes with a few of the others—their hardened stares turning to the dark silhouettes of the forest as they braced for battle.

The silence was gnawing. Mocking them.

"You four, follow the blood," Chereth said, gesturing in Desmond's direction. He took the torch from the older hunter beside him, a resolute clench to his jaw as he tread carefully over the tangle of roots and blossoms.

"The rest of us?" one of the riders called. "Shall we form a perimeter?"

Chereth took a long silence, staring up at the branches above as though he could understand some sinister truth in the frost-coated wood. Then, he held the torch to the base of the tree, patiently waiting for the flames to catch. The fire crackled, smoke carrying a distinct smell as it crept up toward the heavens.

"The rest of us, arm yourselves. We'll burn the bitch out of hiding."

IF YOU ENJOYED THIS BOOK,
PLEASE CONSIDER LEAVING A
REVIEW ON YOUR FAVORITE
PLATFORM-ESPECIALLY
GOODREADS OR AMAZON! THE
IMPACT THIS HAS FOR AUTHORS
CANNOT BE OVERSTATED. THANK
YOU FROM THE BOTTOM OF OUR
TWISTED LITTLE HEARTS!

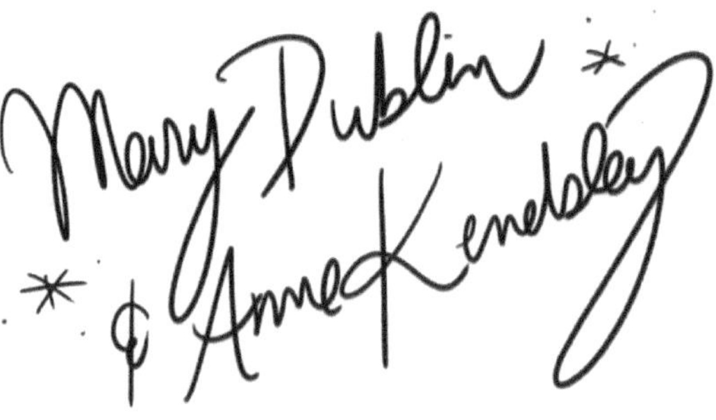

ABOUT THE AUTHORS

JOIN THE STABBY
FAIRY FAM!

Mary Dublin and Anne Kendsley are a best friend
and co-author duo that have been writing and
adventuring together for over twelve years.

When they're not penning the next angsty twist
in their fairycore urban romantasy series, you'll
find them traveling, gaming, and cuddling their
rescue pets, Piper and Clover. They bring a blend
of heart, grit, and magic to everything they
write. With backgrounds rooted in a lifelong
love for immersive fantasy, sci-fi, and the
surreal, Mary and Anne craft stories that both
challenge and enchant.

Learn more at:
HTTPS://AUTHORSDUBLINKENDSLEY.COM/

PRAISE FOR THE SERIES

"IF YOU'RE IN THE MOOD FOR A MAGICAL, FORBIDDEN LOVE ROMANCE WITH A SLOW BURN — THIS IS THE BOOK FOR YOU!
-SHELBY NICOLE, BESTSELLING AUTHOR OF
THE GROVE HOLLOW SERIES™

"ONE OF THE BEST FANTASY BOOKS I'VE EVER READ. THE BANTER AMONG THEM IS REFRESHING IN A STORY THAT COMBINES THE ETHEREAL BEAUTY OF THE FAIRY FANTASY WORLD WITH THE THREAT OF REAL MONSTERS. IT'S LIKE THE PERFECT COMBINATION OF MURDER, MYSTERY, ROMANCE AND MAGIC."
-JULIA, GOODREADS

"IT'S A WORLD YOU WILL WANT TO STAY IN FOREVER... TO ANYONE MISSING SAM AND DEAN WINCHESTER, FEELS THE PULL OF OLD MAGIC ON THEIR FAIRY SOULS, FEELS THEIR BLOOD POUNDING AT THE THOUGHT OF HUNTING EVIL WITH A SHOTGUN AND A KNIFE, OR EVEN JUST LONGS TO FALL IN LOVE... PICK THIS BOOK UP."
-CORTNIE, GOODREADS

"DUBLIN AND KINDSLEY MASTERFULLY BALANCE ROMANCE, SUSPENSE, AND FANTASY IN A TALE THAT ASKS: WHAT ARE WE WILLING TO SACRIFICE FOR LOVE, FREEDOM, AND A FUTURE WE WERE NEVER MEANT TO HAVE? FANS OF SUPERNATURAL, DEEP CHARACTER ARCS, AND DARK ENCHANTING WORLD-BUILDING WILL DEVOUR THIS BOOK."
-NESSA, GOODREADS

MORE FROM THE

SHOT IN THE DARK

UNIVERSE

SHOT IN THE DARK
BOOK 1 (PUB. 2024)

HUNTED IN THE
SHADOWS
BOOK 2 (PUB. 2025)

LURED IN THE CRIMSON
BOOK 3 (COMING 2026,
PREORDER NOW)

ALL OUR LINKS!
FIND YOUR NEXT READ
& MORE

available at 

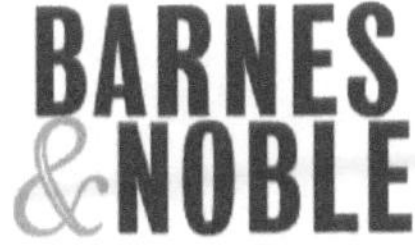

www.ingramcontent.com/pod-product-compliance
Lightning Source LLC
Chambersburg PA
CBHW030148010826
48973CB00002B/782